CHILD OF SORROW

Tennessee Delta Series, Book 3

by
Melinda Clayton

CHILD OF SORROW

by Melinda Clayton
Copyright 2020 Melinda Clayton

This book is a work of fiction. While some of the place names are real, characters and incidents are the product of the author's imagination and are used fictitiously. Any resemblance to events or persons living or dead is purely coincidental.

Cover fonts: Viper Nora, from FontPalace.com, and Open Sans Light, from 1001Fonts.com.

Title inspiration: *The Orphan's Prayer*, a poem by M. G. Lewis.

Library of Congress Control Number: 2020940363
Fiction: Psychological Fiction: Crime
ISBN 13: 978-1-950750-32-0
ISBN 10: 1-950750-32-9
Thomas-Jacob Publishing, LLC, Deltona, Florida

First Printing: June 2020

Thomas-Jacob Publishing, LLC
TJPub@thomas-jacobpublishing.com
USA

For judgment is without mercy to him who has shown no mercy.
James 2:13

Part 1: The Arrest

Chapter 1: Brian Stone

HAD MY CLIENT not tried to kill me that damp April morning, I may have never met Johnathan Thomas Woods. As it was, court had been recessed early, my client quickly subdued by deputies who whisked him back to his cell while I adjusted my tie and pretended to not be shaken by the incident. And because I'm not used to bicycles parked on my walk-way—and was a bit distracted after having been jumped by a pen-wielding maniac—I nearly died for the second time in as many hours when I tripped over a pedal jutting into my path. Thankfully, the force of my face slamming into pavement was enough to stop my fall.

I have a tendency toward sarcasm when I'm angry.

Such was my mood when I stomped into the lobby of my downtown law office, blood dripping down my cheek and a torn flap of wool—*expensive* wool—flapping about my knee.

"Who the hell left—"

"Shush!"

The hissed order coming from my office manager was enough to stop me mid-sentence. Lena Reynolds is by no means a soft-spoken woman; nevertheless, her tone surprised me. Given my appearance, I'd expected a bit of sympathy.

"What—"

"Hush," she said again, more softly this time, tilting her head toward the seating area opposite her desk. "Watch your language; you'll scare him off. He's a bit skittish, almost left a couple of times, but then sat back down."

I grabbed a handful of Kleenex from the box on her desk, pressing them to my cheek as I followed her gaze. "Skittish? Lena, from what I can see he's a kid, not a horse, although the way he's slumped in that chair makes it hard to tell. What's he doing here? I don't have an appointment, and even if I did, he'd need a parent or guardian here. Is this whose god-damned bike—"

"Brian!" This time her voice was loud enough to penetrate through whatever noise the kid had been listening to through his earbuds. He looked up, a scowl on his face, his eyes hidden in the shadow of a dark blue ball cap with the words *Going Fishing* centered in white over the bill. Shaggy hair curled out from under the cap. Brown, maybe. Maybe blond. It was hard to tell, wet as it was.

"What does he want?" I whispered, leaning close to Lena.

"Says he needs an attorney, is all I know." She reached up and gave me a little push in the small of my back. "You're an attorney. Go see what he wants."

"We really need to work on your people skills," I said, tossing the Kleenex into the garbage can beside her desk and tentatively touching my cheekbone. It didn't seem to be broken, and the bleeding had stopped.

"Me?" she asked, brows raised. "I'm not the one storming in here cursing out a child. I'll go pick up another suit for you while you take care of the kid."

"You're going to leave me alone with him?"

"You're a big boy. I'm sure you can handle it." She retrieved her purse from a drawer before pushing past me and shoving the door open with a hip, hiking boots splashing in puddles as she strode into the drizzly morning.

I looked back at the kid. If I'd had to guess, I'd have said he was around thirteen, maybe fourteen. I'm terrible with kids' ages, but he was old enough to have lost the softness younger kids have, yet young enough to still look vulnerable despite the scowl. Maybe even *because* of the scowl. He wore ripped jeans and a dark gray hoodie, damp about the shoulders, the wires to his earbuds snaking out of his zipped-up collar. On his feet he wore scuffed brown duck boots, not unlike a pair I'd had when I was about his age. They'd been a hot item back then; I didn't know if the same was true now, or if he'd found an old pair in a thrift store somewhere. Judging by the look of them, I'd have guessed the latter. They were also wet, I could see, and an old memory rose out of nowhere: another cold, wet Memphis morning much like this one, and me huddled alone in a doorway.

Refusing to speculate on the memory, I instead walked over to the boy, hand extended. "Brian Stone. Lena says you need an attorney."

He stood to greet me, offering me his own cold, wet hand to shake. "Yeah, I do," he said, his eyes darting to my face, then back down. "I'm John. Johnathan Thomas Woods, but I go by John." Another quick look at me. "But you don't look like I thought you would. You know, like the billboard you have beside the interstate."

I'd paid a fortune for that ridiculous billboard, a decision I'd instantly regretted when I first saw the finished eyesore casting a shadow over the I-240 loop around Memphis. "Yeah," I said. "Well, it's been a rough morning. Which reminds me. Is that your bike outside?"

He nodded, stuffing his fingertips into the front pockets of jeans sitting dangerously low on skinny hips.

"You'd better bring it inside," I said. "Otherwise, it'll likely not be there when you go back for it."

He took a tentative step toward the door before turning to me. "Where should I put it?"

I hesitated, the thought of a dirty, wet bike— particularly *that* dirty, wet bike—leaning against a wall in my office enough to make me grimace. "Better bring it to my office," I said. "Go ahead. I'll wait for you." This day just kept getting worse. "Can I get you something to drink? Water? A Coke? Lena keeps us pretty well stocked in the lounge."

"Do you have coffee?" he asked, pausing at the door.

"Aren't you a little young for coffee?"

He made a sound, something between a laugh and a snort. "I'm a little young for a lot of things," he said, "but that doesn't keep them from happening."

He hurried to get his bike, and I walked to the lounge to make us some coffee.

Chapter 2: Lena Reynolds

IT WAS ABOUT a twenty-minute trip to Brian's place, a rustic old cabin set on nearly two dozen acres just south of President's Island. He'd bought it right about the time he was saving my ass from frying in the electric chair.

That's right. A couple of years ago, I was one of his clients. My older sister Rebecca and I hired Brian when I was charged with the brutal murders of my parents and another sister. I didn't make it easy for him; I'll grant you that. I didn't exactly have a lot of trust for what I'd always known as *the system*, and Brian was about as *system* as you could get with his designer suits and manicured nails. Or at least that was what I thought in the beginning. Over the months we'd spent together huddled over a carved-up wooden table at the jail, I'd come to know a very different Brian and adjusted my attitude accordingly. He's a good guy, one of the best.

As you can see, I'm not rotting on death row. As to whether I *should* be … well, that's a matter of opinion. I can't say for certain I didn't murder my family, since I was stoned out of my mind at that time. But Brian believed me to be innocent, and he's damn near convinced me of the same.

Not only did he save my life, he took me in, moved me right into his little cabin—no, not like *that*; get your mind out of the gutter. Like a friend. Like a … well, like the sort of sibling I always wanted but never had. As for Rebecca, my one surviving sister, I haven't seen her since the trial. She disappeared without even saying goodbye as soon as the verdict was read.

Brian, though, he's been there with me through everything, even gave me a job. Created it for me, really, calling me his office manager although I don't know a thing about computers or typing or much of anything else office related. But that's Brian for you; he looks like a prig, but he's forever looking out for strays.

Speaking of strays, if that boy I left in his office wasn't a stray, I didn't know who was. Jittery as hell, that one, propping his muddy feet on our leather chairs—Brian would have a fit when he saw the evidence—squirming and sighing and rolling his eyes as if waiting for Brian were a colossal waste of his time. He didn't have an appointment, just showed up out of the blue saying he needed an attorney. I'd told him Brian was in court and I had no way of knowing when he'd be back, but he sat his scrawny ass down anyway, determined to wait.

I was surprised to see Brian coming through the door that early, even more surprised at the state he was in. He's usually what I think of as a pretty boy, although he's a few years older than I am. Tall, well built, curly silver hair, impeccably dressed. That's not how he looked when he stormed into the office, however. Dripping wet with torn pants, mud down his front, blood on his face, and a plum-colored bruise already spreading over his cheek, he looked more like the men I used to know lurking down in the river bottoms. With the kid there, I hadn't wanted to ask what happened, but I was sure he'd tell me all about it later. In the meantime, I'd grab a clean suit, pack a first aid kit for him, maybe pick up some pulled pork for lunch. He'd like that.

I turned into the long gravel driveway that led to Brian's cabin, taking care to navigate the ruts and puddles. It was a beautiful piece of land butted right up against Mallard Lake. Brian had bought an old, beat up canoe and loved to unwind by spending long weekend mornings fishing for bluegill, crappie, even catfish, although I've always hated catfish. "Bottom-dwelling trash eaters," my father called them, which may have been the only thing he and I had ever agreed on.

Sometimes I went with Brian; other times, I took long walks by myself. It wasn't unusual to surprise a deer or a rabbit along one of the trails or to occasionally spot a snake—usually just a rat snake, but once while I was walking close to the lake a fat, black water moccasin fell from a tree directly in my path. I screamed so loud Brian heard me from the front porch, scaring me even more than the snake had when he came charging through the brush holding a nine-millimeter handgun cocked and ready.

"Jesus, Lena," he'd said, bending over, hands on knees to catch his breath. "Don't do that. Don't scream unless you're in danger, okay? You scared me half to death."

"I *am* in danger," I replied. "At least I was. Where did it go? Oh, God …"

He straightened and reached for my hand. "I'm sure you scared him off," he said. "Now please, come back with me. It's getting late. You have to be careful, Lena."

Brian believed my life was in danger. After all, someone had murdered most of my family. Since he believed me to be innocent, that meant somewhere out there was a murderer, possibly with his—or her—sights set on me. The fact I'd been at the crime scene but was too stoned to remember what happened only added to the danger.

Most days, I was able to successfully tamp down any fears lurking in the back of my mind. Most days. But something about the rain, the gloom, the chill in the air, spooked me. Brian's land was beautiful, but it was also isolated. That's one of the things we both loved about it. Still, as I parked the car and made my way up the flagstone walk, taking care not to slip, I shivered—and not entirely from the wind. By the time I'd made it up the steps and had my key in the lock, I was more than half convinced someone was watching me, hiding in the stand of pecan trees, maybe, or possibly behind the giant maple across the way.

I gathered Brian's things quickly, locking the door on my way out and literally running to the car. I threw the suit and bag into the back seat before jumping in the front, slamming and locking the door behind me. By the time I'd maneuvered my way back out to the main road, I'd nearly shaken the feeling of being watched.

Nearly, but not quite.

Chapter 3: Brian

BY THE TIME the boy—John—had retrieved his bike and propped it against the wall inside my office, the coffee was ready.

"Lots of sugar," John had said when I asked him how he took it.

"A man after my own heart," I said, handing him a steaming cup, which he immediately wrapped his hands around, hunching over and pulling it close to his chest. "Are you cold? I can't help but notice you're soaked."

He shrugged. "A little, but I'll be okay."

I moved around the desk and sat, observing him a moment before asking, "You like to fish?"

"What?"

"Your hat."

He looked puzzled for a moment. "Oh. I don't know. I've never been."

"You should go sometime. I enjoy it quite a bit."

He didn't respond to that, so I decided to forgo pleasantries and dive right in. "You said you need an attorney. Why would that be?"

"I'm in trouble."

Well, naturally. People don't normally visit defense attorneys unless trouble is somehow involved. I nodded and gestured for him to continue. "Go on."

"I think I'm about to be arrested for killing my foster mom."

Whoa. Here I'd thought maybe he'd been caught shoplifting or jaywalking or … hell, I don't know. I certainly wasn't expecting what he'd said.

"Okay, stop right there. That's serious stuff you're talking about. You know, John, we need a parent or guardian here for this conversation."

"I don't have parents."

I'd suspected as much. "They're not involved at all?"

He shook his head. "Parental rights have been terminated," he said in a voice I assumed was meant to mimic a family court judge. "I'm in an emergency placement right now, because … well, like I said, my foster mom was murdered."

"Who's your caseworker?"

"Do I have to tell you?"

"If you want my help, you have to tell me."

"Well, fuck," he said, letting his head drop back against the chair.

"Bright minds can think of better words," I said, surprising myself with the cliché, irritated with myself for using it. It sounded depressingly prim, not like my mother would have sounded—she could have no doubt taught John a thing or two about vulgar language—but instead like one of the many stiffly coiffed caseworkers who'd rotated through my *own* life in my younger years.

John made that sound again, the snort-laugh sound he'd made earlier. "Dude, I've got bigger things to worry about than language."

"Why don't you give me the name of your caseworker, and I'll make a phone call—"

"Fuck that shit," he said, standing and setting his coffee down on my desk hard enough to slosh it out the sides of the Styrofoam cup. "I know how that works. You call her so you can cover your ass and feel like you've done something. She'll add it to her notes, and the next time they have one of their meetings or staffings or court hearings or whatever the hell they have, she'll run it by the treatment"—he gave the word air quotes—"team and they'll spend two hours talking about which specialist I should see next, and meanwhile, no one helps me and nothing changes. Like I said, fuck that shit."

For the first time, his eye contact was steady. And his eyes were gray, I noticed. No, not gray, but a light, almost ethereal silver. Another disconnected memory: laughing, stumbling, dangerously drunk.

Where the hell had that come from?

"Wait," I said, stretching out a hand to stop him. He flinched, and I quickly withdrew. "I want to help you," I said, "but you're a minor. I can't help you without permission from your caseworker. Surely you know that."

"Ah, God." He took off the ball cap and scrubbed a hand through his hair—blond, after all— before shoving the cap back on, yanking it low over his forehead. "Her name is Kathy Stein, but she doesn't know," he said, dropping heavily back into his seat with his hands over his face, seemingly deflated. "I mean, I don't think she knows I'm going to be arrested. Or maybe she does. Probably she does—she always knows everything—but she hasn't said anything to me about it."

"I can't help you unless she's here. We'll call her together."

I watched his chest rise and fall with a deep breath. "Okay, but …"

"What?"

"Could we maybe call her later, like say three-thirty? Because I'm supposed to be in school right now and if she finds out …" He let his hands drop to his lap.

"Today is your lucky day. I was supposed to be in court, but since my client tried to kill me, I'm here for the rest of the day. Head on to school and come back at three-thirty. Then we'll give her a call."

"Someone tried to kill you? Really?"

"With an ink pen."

"Dude, that's cool."

"You and I clearly have different ideas of what constitutes cool."

He smiled for the first time, looking simultaneously younger and older. "Oh, I almost forgot. I can pay you. I have a job helping some old guy with his yard. How much do you charge, anyway?" He shifted to one side, pulling a worn-looking wallet from his back pocket. "I've got two hundred I was saving for a PlayStation. Is that enough?"

"Keep your money," I said, oddly touched. "Let your caseworker and me worry about that. And for God's sake, keep that somewhere safe. You don't need to be wandering around downtown with that kind of money in your pocket."

"That's what Heather says, too," he said, struggling to stuff the wallet back into his sagging back pocket.

"Who's Heather?"

"My friend. At least, she has been. Right now, she's acting like a retard."

I winced at the offensive word. "You know, that's not the best word—"

"I'm telling you I'm about to go to jail for murder, and all you're worried about is my *language*? Dude, seriously?"

Fair enough. I'd let it go for now, but if we were going to be spending any amount of time together, he was going to need to expand his vocabulary.

"Hey, is there somewhere ..." He glanced around the office. "I mean, since I'm supposed to be in school, I don't really have anywhere ..."

"School would be somewhere."

"I don't want to get into all that right now, okay?"

"So you want to just hang out here instead."

"Forget it, man." He stood again. "I'll be back at three-thirty."

"Hold on; sit down. I'm sure we can arrange something." He sat, balanced on the edge of his seat. "As far as I'm concerned, you can stay. But you'll have to tell your caseworker you skipped school to come see me. If we're going to do this, we're going to be honest about it."

"Okay. Whatever. I just really need a place to crash. I don't think she'll get too upset with me if you're here when I tell her."

"Let me make a quick phone call."

He jumped up again, clearly alarmed. "You mean right now? I have to tell her now? I thought you meant when we call this afternoon. No way I'm telling her now, man. She'll make me go to class. I *hate* school—"

Did the kid ever manage to sit through an entire conversation? His constant jumping up and down was enough to make me dizzy. "Relax. You'll talk with her later. I need to talk with her now. How else are we going to set up an appointment?"

"What if she comes here to drag me to school?"

"You saw the billboard. I looked charming, right?"

He blew through his lips, making a raspberry sound. The kid was a veritable library of oral noises. "More like sleazy."

Ouch. "It got you here, didn't it? Whatever works to get the job done."

"You think she'll let me stay?"

"I'm betting on it." I hoped I sounded convincing. "You can wait in the lounge. It's right across the hall. Help yourself to more coffee; the sugar is in the cabinet above the coffee maker. I'll be with you in a minute." He left, and I made a mental note to check the utensil drawer later, then pulled out my cell and selected Lena's number.

"What's up, boss?"

"How close are you to the office?"

"Ten minutes, maybe twelve. Longer now that I've had to pull over to answer my phone. Why do you ask?"

"Can you make a detour?"

"I'm planning to pick us up some lunch, if that's what you need."

"Add another order to whatever you pick up. And could you swing by a store? Get a sweatshirt, some sweatpants? Maybe some socks? I'll pay you back."

"Let me guess. For the kid?"

"He's soaked, Lena. And cold."

"I know. I'll take care of it. I'm guessing we'll have the pleasure of his company for the afternoon?"

"It's looking that way."

"This should be interesting."

"Indubitably."

"What are we about to get into, Brian?"

What, indeed? I ended my call with Lena and looked up the number for Mrs. Kathy Stein of the Department of Human Services. Summoning every ounce of boyish charm I could muster after the morning I'd had—thank God she couldn't see me, with dried blood on my face and a torn pant leg flapping about my knee—I set about talking Mrs. Stein into letting John stay at my office until the three of us could meet later in the afternoon.

Chapter 4: Johnathan Thomas Woods

(But I go by John.)

I WASN'T SURE what to think about the dude. I mean, on the one hand, he let me stay in his office instead of making me go to school, which was cool. And his secretary or whoever she was brought me lunch and some clothes I'd never wear again. White tube socks? Seriously? But it was still nice of them, and I guessed they were both too old to know what people my age wear these days.

He was kind of a smartass, too. Don't get me wrong—I'm a smartass, so I didn't mind that. I liked it. That was another point on the plus side.

But he was obsessed with my language. "Bright minds can think of better words." For real? I was going to prison for *murder,* dude. Who gave a flying fuck about my language? What, I might offend the psychopath in the cell next door? I didn't know what that was about, but it was annoying as hell. Oh, excuse me. As *heck.* I wouldn't want to offend anyone.

If we were going to be spending any amount of time together, he was going to need to chill out about my vocabulary. That was definitely a point for the minus side.

He wasn't charging me, though, so that was a plus. I'd been saving up for a PlayStation for like half my life; every time I almost had enough money, someone stole it. Heather thought it was stupid for me to want the PS4, since I could have bought a PS2 for under a hundred, but what she didn't understand was that for once in my life I wanted something new. Everything I owned was used, from my shoes to the stupid *Going Fishing* hat Mr. Stone asked me about. I was more of a beanie kind of guy, like maybe one from Neff, or even one from American Eagle, but that's not what Faith brought home from the local Goodwill, and as she said at the time, beggars can't be choosers, which was why instead of looking like a kid with some kind of style, I got asked if I liked to fish. I was a beggar.

On the minus side, he looked like what Jimmy Turner, a kid from my last school, would have called a soy boy. Kind of soft. Then again, Jimmy Turner called *me* a soy boy, and Jimmy Turner was an asshole. Besides, Mr. Stone was almost stabbed to death in court but managed to get away with just a cut on his cheek and a skinned knee. That was pretty badass, if you asked me. I only wish I could have seen the fight.

The main thing was, it seemed like he believed me. He took me seriously, or at least he acted like he did, and when you're a kid with more caseworkers than friends, that's pretty dope. And I did tell him the truth, mostly, when I could.

I rolled over and turned on the lamp beside my bed. One good thing about my emergency placement was that I had my own room. The people were okay, too. Kind of old. Quiet. They didn't say much, but that was okay with me. When I first got there, the foster mother told me the room they gave me used to be her son's room, but he was grown now and living somewhere in California with a wife and kids of his own. She looked a little sad when she said it, which made me feel bad for her in a way, so I had to remind myself that wasn't my problem. She probably thought taking in foster kids would help make up for her own kid being gone, but I couldn't get caught up in that kind of drama. I couldn't replace someone's kid, and I'd be shipped off to some other home before long, anyway.

Or to prison.

I sat up and pulled the envelope out of my back pocket, being careful not to tear it. It was the only thing my mother had given me when she dropped me off at the local office of the Department of Human Services. Just a regular old white envelope, one of the longer ones like people use to mail bills in, it was frayed all around the edges and along the creases; fuzzy little bits of lint fell off whenever I unfolded it, which I hardly ever did. I didn't unfold it then, either, because I didn't need to. I probably didn't even need to keep it anymore, since I'd finally used what was in it, but I kept it anyway because it was all I had left of my mom.

I knew people thought she hadn't loved me. Most of the time, I thought that, too. Hell, she said it to me often enough. *God, you're the worst thing that ever happened to me.* She was right about that, so I couldn't really be too upset about it, could I? If it hadn't been for me, she'd have finished her degree and gotten the job she'd always wanted. She'd be an accountant somewhere on Wall Street instead of cleaning houses for rich people. She'd live in a penthouse suite and own a Mercedes instead of living in a fifth-wheel behind some crackhead's mobile home in Frazier and taking the city bus to work down in Germantown.

She'd had to give up all her dreams when she ended up pregnant and alone, and I can see why that would make a person angry. I can see how it would make a person hate everybody, even that person's own kid. Even if that kid was me. But then I'd look at that envelope and know she hadn't really hated me. Not quite, anyway. She'd felt something for me, something besides hate. Not love, maybe, but something. Otherwise, she wouldn't have given it to me. Right?

That envelope was one of the things I hadn't been totally honest with Mr. Stone about, but I couldn't see how that mattered. It never had before.

Chapter 5: Brian

"BILL, THIS IS Brian. Brian Stone." I switched the phone to my left ear and reached for the dossier I'd begun compiling on Mr. Johnathan Thomas Woods.

"What can I do for you, Brian? Is something wrong with Lena?"

"No, Lena's fine. Doing really well, in fact. She makes a hell of an office manager. Aside from, you know, not knowing how to type. Or file. Or … manage."

On the other end of the line, Bill Frazier chuckled. "I doubt she got much practice typing down in those river bottoms. She makes a mean cup of coffee, though. Used to, anyway, back when she came and spent time with us. We let her work kitchen duty since she wasn't high risk. Couldn't cook worth a damn, but the coffee made up for it."

"She makes coffee? She's lived with me for over two years—hard to believe, isn't it?—and I had no idea. She's hidden that skill from me."

"Well, good for her," said Bill. "You're a grown man. Make your own damn coffee. Now, what can I do for you?"

"I hear you're retiring soon."

"You hear right. Did you get your invitation? They're giving me a little retirement party up this way."

"I did, and I'll be there with bells on."

"Leave off the bells," he said, "or the invitation's off. I've seen enough craziness during my career to last a lifetime. What is it about you and those damn bells, anyway?"

We laughed, as we always did, enjoying the familiarity of an old joke.

"What are your plans for retirement?" I asked, the question friendly but my intention not entirely innocent.

"Oh, fishing, hunting. The usual. Why do you ask? And don't tell me you're just being polite. Get to it, Brian, before I die of old age."

"Have you ever thought about doing investigative work?"

"What the hell do you think I've been doing the past forty years?"

"I mean freelance. On your own."

Bill exhaled loudly. "Oh, a time or two. What cop doesn't? But I'm getting a little long in the tooth for something like that now."

"What if I told you I have a fourteen-year-old boy who's being investigated for the murder of his foster mother, and I believe he's innocent?"

Another exhale. "Well, damn, Brian."

"Just think about it, okay?"

"Hell, no, I'm not going to think about it. I'm going to think about sitting out in my skiff with a fishing pole, which is what a man my age ought to be thinking about."

"Parental rights terminated six years ago. No other family. Came in my office today soaked from rain and freezing cold. Pulled out two hundred dollars he'd earned from mowing yards and said he'd pay me to represent him."

"Neighbor of mine caught a catfish must have weighed forty pounds the other day," said Bill. "Invited us over for a fish fry. Best damned hushpuppies I ever tasted."

"I know you're a couple of counties away, but you may have heard about it on the news," I said. "I'd forgotten about it, but talking with his caseworker today, began to remember. Body of a middle-aged woman found rolled up in a tarp in a dumpster off Lamar Avenue back in January. Word at the time was that her throat was slit first, and then she was hogtied with a belt."

Silence. Then, "I might remember that. Security cameras at the dumpster were out of order. Busted lenses and full of spider nests. And they think the kid did it, huh?"

"Bill, this kid isn't a buck twenty soaking wet. No way he could have done all that. Hell, he can't even drive."

Bill grunted. "Plenty of ways around that. Wouldn't have to be too big to sneak up on someone from behind. And it wouldn't be too difficult to hogtie a dead woman. Makes you wonder why, though, doesn't it? Why tie up someone who's already dead?"

"I bet you'll find out."

"Why are you so convinced he's innocent, Brian?"

"He was willing to give me his PlayStation money to defend him." It was more than that, of course, but not something I could explain to Bill.

"Well, that's a sure sign, if ever I've seen one." I could almost see him rolling his eyes. "Has he been charged?"

"Nope," I said. "He's not even officially named as a suspect."

"Then why in the hell—"

"He's not officially named, but that doesn't mean he's not being investigated. You know how that works."

"Foster mother, you say?"

"That's right."

"Any indication there was trouble between them? Signs of abuse? Do you have access to his records?"

"Those are the sorts of questions I'd expect a private investigator to ask."

This time, his exhalation nearly took out my eardrum. "It's not that simple, Brian. I've got the education, and God knows the experience; that's not a problem. But there's an exam I'd need to take."

"Is that it?"

"No, I'd have to be affiliated with a law office or P.I. company." He hesitated. "Or start a P.I. company of my own."

"I vote for the latter. You've got more experience than anyone I know, Bill."

"Damn it to hell, Brian, why am I even listening to you? Do you know it's turkey season? I've got a bow I haven't used in five years, I've been so busy."

"When does the season end? May, right? It'll probably take you that long to apply and take the test. I can help you incorporate. It's not my area, but it's easy enough to do, and I won't even charge you for it."

"Mighty charitable of you."

"You're welcome." I couldn't stop smiling, and I was sure he heard it in my voice. "Why don't you come for dinner Saturday? Bring Patty with you. Lena would love to see you, and I'd love to show you the place. You and I can start the incorporation paperwork, and I'll have you sign a non-disclosure agreement. That way, I can fill you in on our boy."

"Our boy, huh?"

"You won't be sorry, Bill."

"I might be, if y'all are the ones cooking."

"We'll order from Top's."

"Now you're trying to bribe me."

"Is it working?"

"Hell, at this point I'd agree to anything to get you to shut up. It'll just be me, though. Patty's going out with some of the women from church. Besides, she stopped wanting to hear anything about cases a long time ago."

"Can't blame her for that, but tell her we'll miss her. We'll plan to eat around six, but come anytime you want. We'll take the canoe out and go fishing. I've got plenty of gear, so don't worry about bringing anything."

We firmed up plans before disconnecting, and I scooped John's dossier into my briefcase. Lena had already left for the day, and I was anxious to get home, worried, as always, about her safety.

Even so, I felt compelled to stand alone for a minute in the parking garage before entering my car. I turned to the west, relishing the cold wind off the Mississippi, grateful for the invisible bonds that kept me tethered to the good people of this world in spite of the evil I knew sometimes walked the streets.

Chapter 6: Brian

"BRIAN AND LENA, I'd tell you the food is delicious, but we all know neither one of you can cook worth a damn. Thank God for Top's." Bill sucked the barbecue sauce off his fingers with a loud *smack*.

"I can cook," Lena said, reaching across the table to hand him an extra napkin. "I just have a different technique. I'm used to cooking over a trash barrel. It adds flavor. None of that fancy kitchen stuff for me."

Bill laughed. "I'm sure it's wonderful that way, but I think I'll pass." He wiped his mouth before turning to me. "This is one hell of a place you have here."

"Thanks, Bill." We'd hiked the perimeter before taking the canoe out for a couple hours of fishing. Bill would be going home with a Styrofoam cooler full of fish, much to his delight. It had been a good day—an excellent day—until we'd arrived back at the cabin and I'd caught a glimpse of something out of the corner of my eye. Bill hadn't noticed it, distracted as he was by his catch, and I didn't bring it to his attention, not wanting to ruin the pleasant evening. But it had been gnawing at me ever since. I did my best to put it out of my mind and focus on the conversation at hand.

"Getting out of that condo in the city has definitely been good for me," I said. "It's hard to remember what I ever saw in it. It seems like a different lifetime."

"It was," said Bill, "and you were a different man."

I nodded. It was true; for better or worse, I was a very different man.

"I never have understood how anyone can live with all that traffic and noise," Bill continued, "and all those *people*. Give me the country any day of the week. This is just about the perfect size, too. Plenty of room to roam, but not so big you can't take care of it. You've got yourself a gem, Brian."

I glanced around the room, appreciating through Bill's eyes the oak floors and shiplap walls. I'd been excited to discover the original shiplap hiding behind cheap paneling someone had installed in the sixties or seventies, back when dark paneled walls were in vogue. I'd been even happier when I pulled back filthy scalloped carpet to reveal wooden floors in excellent condition. A coat of whitewash on the walls and a soft satin finish on the floors had been all that was needed to bring out the natural beauty of the cabin.

Bill pushed his empty plate aside. "Did I get everything signed you needed me to sign?"

"You did. I'll file the paperwork Monday. Would you care for some ice cream and strawberries? Lena and I found some straight off the vine at the farmers market this morning."

"Sounds good, but I'm afraid I'm full to capacity. Now, tell me about your boy before I fall asleep in this chair. Good fishing, good meal, good company. Next thing you know, I'll be snoring."

I stood to clear the dishes, but Lena waved me away. "I'll get them," she said. "Bill's right. He's got a long drive home, so you'd better share whatever you need to share. I've got homework to do, anyway."

"Homework?" Bill tilted his head to look up at her. "What kind of homework?"

"I'm finishing up my GED," she said over her shoulder as she stacked plates in the dishwasher. "You know I never graduated high school. Seems like a good time to get that taken care of."

"Well, I'll be," said Bill. "You're full of surprises, Lena."

Lena smiled but didn't answer. She was never fully comfortable on the receiving end of a compliment. While she packed leftovers for Bill, I reached to the shelf behind me and grabbed the kid's file. I'd avoided discussing the case out in the canoe, preferring instead to hear about Bill's upcoming retirement and subsequent plans. I tried as much as possible to avoid work discussions out on the lake; it seemed almost sacrilegious to bring the ugliness I encountered in my professional life back to my sanctuary. But it was getting late, and I knew Patty would start to worry if Bill had to make the long drive home too late at night.

"Name is Johnathan Thomas Woods," I began. "Goes by John. He's fourteen years old. Been in and out of the system most of his life, but parental rights weren't terminated until six years ago. Mother's rights, I should clarify. According to the mother, father is deceased. Died in a car accident while she was pregnant."

"Siblings?"

"None. First came to the attention of the Department of Human Services when a woman called the police one night after hearing her next-door neighbor's baby scream for hours. When the police arrived, the mother was nowhere to be found. Baby boy—three months old, it was later determined—was found naked, covered in vomit and feces, in a roach-infested cardboard box set in the middle of a mattress on the floor. A baby bottle half full of spoiled milk was tipped on its side, dripping into the mattress."

"Emergency foster placement?"

"Hospital first. He was dehydrated and malnourished, not to mention covered with bug bites, many of them infected. Spent a few days there before being placed."

"Where was mother during this time?"

"According to witnesses, in a bar. Until closing time, anyway, at which point she stumbled home with the bartender. Apparently, she forgot she had a kid at home."

"Let me guess. She completed parenting classes and alcohol and drug treatment, and a few months later the baby was returned."

"You got it."

"Until it happened again."

"And again. They continued that cycle for the next eight years. He'd go back home until someone else made a report. Then he'd go back to foster care."

"What finally led to termination?"

"She told the Department to keep him."

Bill uttered a long string of profanity under his breath, apologizing as Lena appeared carrying a tray outfitted with two cups of coffee, spoons, sugar, and cream.

"Believe me, I've heard worse," she said, setting the tray down and handing each of us a cup. "Even said worse to you, Bill, and you know it. Coffee's decaffeinated, so don't worry it'll keep you awake."

"Thank you, darlin'," said Bill, while I sat openmouthed.

"Well, I'll be damned. Bill said you made good coffee, but I told him you'd never revealed that secret to me."

Lena winked, placing a hand on Bill's shoulder. "Well, Bill is Bill, and you're you. Now get back to work."

"Wow," I said, watching her leave the room. "Okay, then. Where were we? Oh, right. Mom told the Department to keep John." I sipped the coffee. Bill was right; it was delicious. "He's been in multiple placements over the past six years," I continued, "but none of the moves were due to behavioral issues. One family moved for the wife's job. Another decided one foster child was enough, so John had to go. Another was found guilty of committing welfare fraud. You know how it goes."

Bill stirred cream into his coffee, taking a loud slurp before replying. "How long was he in this last one? The one where foster mom was murdered?" And then, "Mmm-mm-mmm. Told you she made a mean cup of coffee."

"So you did," I said. "I really can't believe you two." I shook my head in mock dismay. "But to answer your question, he'd been with Faith Irving for close to a year. About six months before she was killed, Ms. Irving—who was divorced, by the way—agreed to take in another kid. A girl this time. Teenager a year older than John."

"An unrelated teenaged boy and girl in the same home? And they thought this was a good idea?"

I shrugged. "The girl needed somewhere to go, and the caseworker was trying to keep her in the same school district. She continued to look for a more appropriate placement, but they aren't always easy to come by. But it's interesting you ask, because that's one reason John has come under suspicion."

"What do you mean?"

"Foster mom and caseworker were a little worried John and Heather—Heather Renfro is her name—were getting too close. Physically close, if you know what I mean. Foster mom came home from work one day and caught them in an embrace on the couch. They were fully clothed, but according to her, they looked guilty. The caseworker, Kathy Stein, had been actively looking for a more suitable placement for Heather."

"So John—what?—flew into a rage at the possibility of losing his girlfriend and killed her? This kid who has no history of behavioral problems? Is that what they think?"

"I didn't say he had no behavioral problems," I corrected. "I said he'd never been *moved* due to behavioral problems. He's a status offender. Ran away a couple of times, skips school more than he attends, fights with other kids, caught sneaking vodka from the pantry. Took one foster dad's car for a joyride. That kind of thing."

"I thought you said he couldn't drive."

"I should amend that to say he can't *legally* drive."

Bill looked heavenward before asking, "What else do we know about him?"

"He has a reputation among his teachers and peers for having a temper. He also has a past diagnosis of Oppositional Defiant Disorder but was discharged from therapy several months ago when the therapist deemed him not amenable to treatment."

"Meaning?"

"He refused to attend."

"So he's an angry kid," said Bill. "Sounds like he has a right to be. What do they have to go on?"

"Apparently there are witnesses claiming John and Ms. Irving had a contentious relationship. Some say she'd grown afraid of him, but if that's true, she never reported it to the caseworker. There are also reports he may have made threats against her, although the police haven't shared the nature of those threats. And he hasn't been charged with a delinquent act. Not yet. But he's a smart kid; he knows the police aren't following him around just to say hello. And he's right. Mrs. Stein, the caseworker, has already been questioned not once, but twice."

"And the girl? Heather? Where does she fit in?"

"As you guessed, the prosecution will no doubt argue that John killed Ms. Irving because she was trying to separate him from Heather. The police may suspect Heather knows something, but she couldn't have physically participated in the murder. She was having her wisdom teeth removed that day; the appointment was at three. Mrs. Stein picked Heather up from school for her appointment at two-thirty, then tried to drop Heather off at home around five-thirty, but Ms. Irving never came to the door. Mrs. Stein tried to call her, but didn't get an answer. She ended up taking Heather home with her. When she still couldn't reach Ms. Irving by seven o'clock, she notified the police. As you know, Ms. Irving's body was found in the dumpster just after eight in the evening."

Bill pulled a small notebook and pen from his back pocket. "Where was John while Heather was with the oral surgeon?"

"He was supposed to be in school part of that time, but he was recorded as absent in the school's attendance system. After school was out ... well, that's a bit of a problem for us." I paused, chewing on my bottom lip a moment before adding, "I'm hoping you can help us with that."

"I'm guessing he has no alibi."

"Says he spent the day wandering around downtown Memphis."

"Alone."

"Of course."

"Any surveillance videos? Witnesses from the streets?"

"That's what I need you for."

"Crime scene?"

"I don't know much yet, but I have an inside source who told me luminol turned Ms. Irving's bathroom blue."

"Murder weapon?"

"Never found."

"Faith Irving's car?"

"Police found it in the garage. It's a detached building, a converted shed of some sort, no windows."

He paused to jot down some notes before flipping the page and firing more questions at me so quickly I struggled to keep up. "Anything captured on video? Cars coming and going? DNA and fingerprints in Ms. Irving's?"

I chuckled. "You know, Bill, if you'd ever decided you'd had enough of chasing down bad guys, you'd have made a great prosecutor."

He grunted. "Would have paid more. Probably better retirement, too. I don't even know why I'm doing this. I should be home watching reruns of *Matlock* right about now."

"It's in your blood," I said, and he rolled his eyes. "You can't give it up. But to your questions, I don't know how many tests have been completed at this point, and since John isn't officially my client yet, I don't have access to much. Regardless, John's DNA and fingerprints would be expected. He lived there for nearly a year. I do know that Ms. Irving outweighed John by a good thirty pounds. That's according to Mrs. Stein, the caseworker. Even if he'd jumped her from behind, he'd have had a hell of a time loading her up and tossing her body into a dumpster."

"I've seen crazier things happen." Bill rubbed his chin, the sound raspy in the quiet room. "Maybe he was working with someone else."

"If so, I have no doubt you'll find out."

"Tell me something, Brian." He tossed his pen onto the table. "Why are you involved? He hasn't been charged with anything, but if he is, he'll be given access to an attorney. As you well know, there are funds available for this sort of thing, and there are plenty of attorneys who typically handle these sorts of cases. Cases which, I might add, don't pay quite in the range you're used to."

"John chose me," I said. "He saw my billboard on the interstate."

"God, that awful thing?" He smirked. "I'm surprised it didn't send him running in the opposite direction."

"It's not that bad," I replied.

"Oh, it is," he said, before changing subjects. "They can't pay me, you know. The Department isn't known for hiring private investigators. It's a little outside their budget."

"They won't, but I will."

"And who's going to pay *you*?"

"If he does end up being charged, there are a couple of options I've already discussed with his caseworker. I've had juvenile cases before, so it's not outside my area of expertise."

"And if he doesn't end up being charged?"

"Then the time I've spent will be pro bono. I haven't had a pro bono case in a while, so it's time."

"Are lawyers really required to do that? Seems like I heard that somewhere." He flipped his notebook closed and returned it and the pen to his pocket.

"Not required, no. But strongly encouraged by the American Bar Association. I make enough, Bill. I can afford to give some back."

"This is quite a lot to give."

"Says the man who anonymously paid for Lena's therapy most of her adult life," I replied.

"Hush, now," he said, looking over his shoulder. "You have no way of knowing that."

"I do now. I doubt you'd have been so quick to shush me if I'd been wrong." I smiled.

He made a show of looking at his watch. "It's time for me to head home, Brian." He pushed against the table and shoved his chair back. "What's next? Where do we go from here?"

"How soon can you take the exam?"

"I can't send in the application until the incorporation paperwork goes through. How long will that take?"

"Should have it within a week."

"So we're looking at two, three weeks maybe. Will be even longer before I can start working, depending on how long it takes to get my exam scores back. And there's always a chance I won't pass it."

"You'll pass it, and that gives you plenty of time to bag a turkey."

He stood, picking up his empty coffee cup. "That it does. Now let me put this in the kitchen and go tell Lena goodbye, and I'll be on my way."

I stood along with him. "Don't forget your fish."

"Not a chance. I ain't about to leave 'em here for y'all to ruin."

Chapter 7: Lena

BRIAN HAD BEEN on the porch swing for nearly an hour when I could no longer resist the temptation to join him.

"Here," I said, handing him a cup of hot cocoa. "And here." I sat next to him and spread an afghan over our laps. "It's turned cold out here."

"Has it? I hadn't noticed." His breath was visible in the unseasonably cool night air. Somewhere off in the distance an owl hooted, and I shivered forcefully enough to bring Brian back from wherever he'd been. "You okay?" he asked.

"Just chilly," I said. "What about you? You okay?"

He put an arm around my shoulders and pulled me close. "I am," he said. "At one time, that seemed unimaginable, but I really am okay."

I laughed. "Ditto." A few years ago I'd been homeless, living on the banks of the Mississippi River, never knowing where my next meal would come from but with a fairly good idea what I might have to barter in exchange for it.

Brian grinned; I could see his teeth gleaming in the soft light spilling from the kitchen window. "We're quite a pair, aren't we? I'm glad you're here."

"Either you're *really* glad I'm here," I said, pushing away from him, "or you have a gun strapped around your waist."

He laughed. "I am really glad you're here, but, yes, that's a Glock. I took it with me to the lake today in case of snakes and just haven't taken it off yet. Not that you're not gorgeous—"

"Okay, Brian, whatever you say."

"Because you are."

I swatted at him before leaning back against his shoulder.

I'd moved in with Brian the same day the jury found me innocent of murder. Or if not innocent, exactly, at least not guilty. Had he not extended the invitation, I don't know where I'd be right now. Back down in the bottoms, I suppose, waking up in strange places with strange people, my head pounding and my mouth sour. Even so, I hadn't wanted to accept the offer, not at first. But I was tired. I literally didn't have it in me to hitchhike back down there, scavenging for food and crawling into bushes to sleep, jolting awake with every sound, imagined or not. I initially agreed to one night, which became one week, and then one month, and now here we are.

My transition from river rat to Brian's roommate wasn't always smooth sailing, of course. I had to get past his pretty-boy looks and fancy vocabulary, and he had to get past my … well, I'd been living in the bottoms for a long time. He had to get past a lot of stuff. And yet, through it all, he's always felt *familiar* to me, and I believe I have to him, as well.

It may be hard for someone who hasn't walked in my shoes to understand, but my affection for Brian isn't sexual, nor is his for me. Of that, I'm sure. We tease each other from time to time, but I've been so damaged sexually that if I ever did—God forbid—feel attracted to Brian, I'd run for the hills. Or, more realistically, the bottoms. I have no reference for what constitutes a healthy sex life, and at my age, I no longer even care. Why on earth would I want to engage in something that's caused me nothing but pain? I have safety and familiarity and comfort, and that's all I need. It's all I ever wanted to begin with.

In the early days with Brian, I often wondered if we had past lives, and if we did, did we spend each life in a subconscious search for the people we'd known in the previous ones? That was how my relationship with Brian felt to me, as weird as that might sound.

I'd spent a lot of time thinking about such things, but I'd never voiced the thoughts aloud. Hell, I'd done so many drugs down in those bottoms I wasn't even sure my brain worked the way it was supposed to. Maybe the idea of a previous life was the only way I could make sense of the current one. Or maybe my thoughts were nothing more than the ramblings of a half-crazy woman.

"Do you ever think," Brian was saying, "we carry relationships with us from one life to the next?"

"You're crazy," I said, but I smiled.

"Samsara," he said. "The Hindu belief that births and deaths are cyclical, linked by reincarnation. It's fascinating stuff, really."

"I was just thinking about that."

"Synchronicity," he replied, giving me a shoulder bump.

"You and your big words," I said. "But I really was, and I know what you mean. Sometimes you meet someone you feel you already know."

"Exactly," he nodded. "Almost as if you recognize them from somewhere else when you can't possibly."

"Is that why you're so bent on helping this kid? John? You feel as if you know him?"

"Maybe," he said. "That might be part of it."

"And the other part?"

He turned toward me in the dark. "I don't trust anyone else to do it the way it should be done. He deserves someone who will fight for him."

"You're a good man, Brian." I patted his leg.

"I don't know about that, Lena." He set the swing in motion again. "Sometimes it's hard to know whether what you're doing is good or bad."

I knew Brian grieved the loss of friends he'd known before we met, but he'd never told me the whole story. I suspected it was that to which he referred.

"What's the intent, Brian? To help or to hurt?"

"To help, of course."

"Then it's the right thing to do." I squeezed his hand.

He squeezed mine back. "If only it were that easy, but it rarely ever is. The road to hell, and all that. Just ask Mississippi catfish how they feel about Asian carp."

"You lost me with that one."

He laughed. "It's all right. We'll watch the documentary sometime."

"It sounds fascinating."

"I detect a note of sarcasm."

"Just a note? Your hearing must be off." I shivered again and pulled the afghan closer to me.

"You're freezing," he observed. "Go inside. I'll be in shortly."

I didn't want to leave him, but I sensed he wanted to be alone. "At least wrap up," I said, slipping out from under the afghan and rearranging it around his shoulders. "We don't need you coming down with pneumonia and heading into your next life too soon."

"I'll do my best not to croak," he promised. "Now go inside and warm up. Your teeth are chattering somewhere in the prestissimo range."

An hour or so later I was finally warm, drifting into sleep, when I heard the creak of the front door closing, followed by the click of the lock and the whispery scuff of Brian's steps as he entered his bedroom and quietly closed the door.

Chapter 8: Lena

THE NEXT TIME I was awakened, it was to a soft knock.

"Breakfast is ready," Brian said through my door. "Pancakes, sausage links, and lots of hot coffee. Can I come in?"

I stretched, inhaling the delicious aromas of coffee and maple syrup. Opening my eyes, I took in the bright slant of sun across the bedroom floor. "Sure," I replied, sitting up and rubbing my face. "What time is it?"

Brian cracked open the door and poked his head in. "A little after ten. Are you hungry?"

"Ten! Good Lord, I haven't slept that late since … well, ever, unless I was passed out." I stood and began fluffing pillows and tugging bedclothes into place. "Why didn't you wake me sooner?"

"I assumed you needed sleep. Did I keep you awake last night?"

"You mean by sitting alone on the porch in the freezing cold with a gun and staring into space for hours? No, not really. Why would that bother me?"

"I'm sorry," he said, offering me a lopsided grin. "I didn't mean to worry you. My schedule is sometimes off. Sit up all night, sleep all day, eat cookies for breakfast, drink beer for lunch …. There was never anyone around to answer to until now."

"It's fine, Brian." I grabbed a ponytail holder from my nightstand and tried to wrestle my hair into submission. "I just want you to be okay."

"I am," he said. "Really."

"Did you sleep at all?"

"Are you kidding? A body doesn't look this good without sleep." He held his arms wide and looked down at himself.

I stopped fiddling with my hair to take a good look at him. Brian is always a handsome man, but that morning he had dark circles under his eyes and his silver curls, usually carefully arranged, were wild about his head. "I think you need some more sleep," I said.

"Hurtful."

"So what are your answers?"

"What?"

"Your answers. You said there was never anyone around to answer to. What kept you up all night?"

"Come and fix yourself a plate before everything gets cold, and then we'll talk." He closed the door softly on his way out.

I threw on jeans and a t-shirt, and after a quick stop to brush my teeth and wash my face, joined Brian in the breakfast nook, where a steaming cup of coffee awaited me. "Thank you for this," I said, reaching to fork a couple of pancakes and transfer them to my plate. "Now get to it. What kept you up all night?"

"Nothing like a little small talk to break the ice."

"I don't have all day," I said, stuffing half a sausage link into my mouth. "I've already slept half of it away."

Brian poured himself a glass of orange juice and took a long drink before setting the glass down and staring at me for an uncomfortable length of time.

"What?" I wiped my mouth on the back of my hand. "What is it?" I reached for a napkin.

"Not that," he said. "You're fine. But I have a question I need to ask you."

"Okay. What?"

"Have you noticed anything weird lately? Anything … alarming?"

"I assume you mean aside from your own behavior?"

"Cute, but yes."

I thought for a moment. "No, but it might help if I knew which direction you're going. What do you mean, exactly?"

"Have you seen anyone on the place?"

"You mean here? This place?"

"Yes."

I thought back to the feeling I'd had of being watched earlier in the week. "No. I haven't seen anything, but I felt … I don't know … afraid, to be honest. Earlier this week, when I came home to get you a different suit after you fell on the sidewalk."

"Tripped," he corrected. "On a damn bicycle. But that's beside the point. Afraid? Why? Had something happened?"

"No. I feel ridiculous even mentioning it. I just felt as if … as if someone were watching me. It was rainy and gloomy, and I got spooked. But nothing happened, aside from me running to the car like a maniac to get out of here."

"Why didn't you tell me?"

"Because as I said, nothing happened."

Brian stood and walked to the kitchen window, his back to me, hands in his pockets. "You have to let me know if you feel that way again, okay?"

"Are you listening to me, Brian? Nothing happened."

"But it *could* have," he said, his voice slightly raised. "Promise."

"Fine, I promise. And don't get cranky with me. What's going on?"

"I saw footprints in the pecan grove."

I thought back to that rainy morning, the fear I'd felt, the certainty someone was watching me … *hiding in the stand of pecan trees, maybe, or possibly behind the giant maple across the way.*

"When? Brian, I think you'd better fill me in."

Brian scratched the back of his head, a gesture I recognized as an attempt to buy time in which to formulate his answer. "Yesterday evening, when Bill and I were walking back to the house. Partial prints, impossible to tell the full size, but it looked like some sort of boot with thick tread. There were quite a few of them left in the mud, but dry now, obviously several days old. It looked as if the person who made them had been pacing in circles before standing still for a long time, long enough to sink a little deeper, while facing the cabin."

Gooseflesh pimpled my arms. "You think what I felt was real. Someone was watching me."

"I think it's possible."

I set my fork aside, no longer hungry. "What did Bill say about it?"

"I didn't tell him. I wasn't completely certain that's what I'd seen until I checked again after he left."

"That's why you had the gun last night."

"Yes."

"Brian, who do you think it was?"

"I don't know," he answered, coming back to sit across from me. "A person meets a lot of unsavory characters in my kind of work. It could have been anyone. What bothers me most is we're not easy to find. The cabin isn't visible from the road, so for someone to be here, right in front of the house, watching … Well, whoever it was, they had no business being here."

"You don't think it was random; you think someone came here deliberately to …" I stopped. "To what, Brian? Why do you think they were here?"

"I don't know," he said, but he avoided my eyes as he answered.

"You think they were here for me." I knew it was true as soon as I said it.

"I didn't say that, Lena."

"You didn't have to. Oh, God." It was my turn to stand and walk to the window. Outside, the morning was gorgeous, the cool, misty air of the night before long gone. Wild-growing buttercups and jonquils dotted the fields, creating vivid splashes of yellow against a clear, blue sky. New green leaves unfurled on the grand old trees lining the yard, casting dappled patterns over the field grass. It was impossible to imagine something evil lurking in a place so beautiful. But then I looked across the way, to the stand of pecan trees standing separate, tall and regal, the ground below their thick canopy dark, hidden in shadow. Maybe not so impossible, after all.

Brian came to stand behind me, placing his hands on my shoulders and turning me to face him. "We don't need to overreact," he said. "We just need to be aware. Keep the doors locked at all times, and don't go walking by yourself. I've been meaning to get a security and surveillance system installed since I bought the place. We'll get that done this week. And I have friends in the sheriff's department I can ask to keep an eye out when they're making the rounds. I'll also check with Bill and see if …" He left the thought unfinished.

"See if what? He's heard from Rebecca?" So far as I knew, no one had heard from my sister since she'd disappeared right after the verdict was read, squealing tires on her way out of the parking lot. I certainly hadn't. "You still think she did it, don't you Brian? You think she killed my family."

"What do *you* think?"

"I don't know. I try not to think about it. I don't want to believe she could have done something like that."

"Whether or not it was Rebecca, it's best to be safe," he said. "*Someone* killed your family, and that someone is still out there. I don't want you out here alone, understand? Not until we figure this out. And we need to spend some time today on target practice, if for no other reason than that it's snake mating season."

"More snakes. Wonderful." I let my head fall forward against his chest. "This sucks, every single bit of it. I can't do this to you, Brian. I'll get my own place. It's not fair to expect you—"

"That would be the overreacting part I mentioned," he said, pulling me into a hug. "The only way I want you moving out is if we feel it's too dangerous for you to stay. There are steps we can take to keep that from happening. Now let's get this mess cleaned up so I can teach you how to use a handgun."

Chapter 9: Brian

NOTWITHSTANDING the rocky start to our Sunday, we'd had a good day. Both of us enjoy being outdoors, and both of us are competitive. It didn't take long for Lena to put our morning talk behind her—or at least on the back burner, so to speak—so she could focus on attempting to outshoot me. I had a target nailed to an old, dead tree, and we made up a point system wherein the loser had to buy the winner lunch for a week.

I won, of course; I've had years of experience. But she wasn't half bad—was pretty darn good, in fact. Good enough that I felt much more comfortable in her ability to use a handgun if the need arose. I hoped it never would. I also knew she'd pay me back for the loss. I looked forward with trepidation to the lunches she'd bring me the following week. Lena does not lose gracefully, and she well knows my aversion to corned beef.

We'd ended the day with a couple of grilled steaks, a fresh salad, and a rented movie. Neither of us mentioned the possibility of someone lurking outside, but I noticed as I double-checked door and window locks that Lena wasn't far behind me.

And so the week had gone, peacefully and for the most part uneventfully. Bill registered to take his test, and I continued with my other cases. Wednesday evening our new security and surveillance system was installed, which seemed to bring Lena both comfort and entertainment. I'd ordered surveillance cameras not only outside the cabin, but farther away, around the perimeter of the yard. One was aimed specifically at the pecan grove, and Lena got a kick out of monitoring inquisitive squirrels as they clambered over and around the camera, their furry little faces, unbeknownst to them, freakishly huge on the big screen in my home office.

"This is better than cable T.V.," she'd said that first evening as she sat apparently enraptured by huge squirrel faces. "I'm naming this one Ernie." She pointed to the screen, where a particularly aggressive squirrel seemed to be trying to eat the camera.

"How can you tell them apart?" I asked. "One massive squirrel tongue looks like another."

"Ernie's missing a tooth," she said. "See?"

"I don't know if my heart can take looking that closely again. He's like a furry Godzilla."

"Take my word for it, then," she said. "This is Ernie."

As I've said, it was a typical week, all the way until Friday morning when I discovered not one, but two urchins in my doorway.

To be accurate, Lena was the one who discovered them. We parked in the attached parking garage and entered my office suite through the back, as we did most mornings, so didn't immediately see the kids huddled on the threshold of the front office door. I walked to my office to set down my briefcase, while Lena switched on lights and unlocked doors. I'd just booted up my laptop when she called me.

"Brian, can you come here?"

She didn't sound afraid, so I was more curious than panicked. Still, I hurried to see what she needed, where I was met by two surly-looking kids wearing hoodies and earbuds.

"'S'up?"

I'd worked with enough kids over the years to know John was using a salutation considered appropriate in his teenaged world and not actually inviting me to dine.

"I think that's better asked of you," I said. "What brings you here? Is everything all right?" I'd no sooner finished asking the question than the hooded figure next to him bent over and vomited on my shoes.

"Oh, goodness," said Lena, jumping into action and taking the person's—girl's, I could now see, with the hood pushed back—arm. "Let's get you inside where you can sit down."

"Inside?" My voice nearly squeaked. "She just threw up on my feet and you want to take her *inside*?"

"She needs to sit down, Brian, and you have plenty of other shoes." Lena hurried the girl inside, settling her on the leather couch in my lobby.

Well, of course. Why *wouldn't* you settle a person experiencing obvious intestinal distress onto an expensive leather sofa? In the meantime, I rushed to clean my shoes before they were ruined, then grabbed a bowl from the office kitchen and filled it with water to slosh over the remaining mess on the sidewalk out front. I was stepping outside, barefoot and with my suit pants rolled to my knees, when the girl made retching sounds again. Thankfully, Lena was prepared this time, holding the girl's hair back while positioning a garbage can under her chin. By the time I'd replaced the bowl and given my shoes a final wipe down, the girl was stretched out with her head on a throw pillow, a cold, wet dishcloth from the kitchen spread over her forehead.

"Sorry about your shoes," she said when I sat on the chair across from her. Her eyes were huge and dark, her face thin, chin pointed. She looked frightened, and I felt an immediate affinity towards her, not to mention guilt for having worried more about my shoes and our sidewalk than I had her obvious suffering.

"This is Heather." John was on his knees beside the couch, one arm protectively stretched over the couch arm above the girl's head. "She has an upset stomach."

"So I gathered," I said. "I'll assume that's why you're skipping school again."

He ignored the implied question, saying instead, "We need help."

"I'm an attorney, John, not a doctor."

I didn't quite catch John's mumbled response, but it sounded suspiciously like, "You're also an asshole."

Lena's snicker served to validate my suspicions. "We need to call Mrs. Stein so she can get Heather to a doctor," she said, once she'd finished laughing at my expense.

"I don't need a doctor." Heather struggled to sit up.

"My garbage can begs to differ," said Lena, "but the decision will be Mrs. Stein's. I'll give her a call. You at least need someone to make sure you're getting plenty of rest and fluids."

"No." John jumped to his feet. "Come on, Heather." He grabbed her hands, pulling her to her feet. "I should have known it wouldn't do any good to come here."

The sudden motion was clearly too much for Heather, who clamped a hand over her mouth, prompting Lena to grab the garbage can again, just in time. When she was finished, Lena guided her gently back to the couch.

"Lena, put disinfectant on your office supply list, would you?" I wasn't trying to be a prig, as Lena would say, but I had a full schedule and no time to be sick. No time, in fact, to be dealing with a sick teen in my lobby. I couldn't fathom why John had brought her to my office, or what he thought I could possibly do for her.

"It's not contagious," said John. "She's pregnant."

"John—" Heather covered her face with her hands.

"We have to tell them, Heather. Everyone is going to find out, and that'll make it look even more like I killed Faith. They'll try to say this was my motive."

"Pregnant?" I was clearly a beat behind, but it had taken a moment for John's declaration to sink in. I caught Lena's eye. She looked as stunned as I felt.

"How far along?" she asked, glancing at Heather's flat stomach and narrow waist.

"Three months, I think," Heather answered. "It can't be much longer than that."

"It's okay," said John. "I'm going to take care of her, but you have to keep me out of jail so I can." He stared at me, jaw clenched, chin jutted out, his face a mask of defiance. A face, I couldn't help but think, that was still little-boy smooth. Good God, he was just a child.

"So am I to assume the baby—"

"It's mine," he interrupted. "I know we're just kids, unprotected sex, irresponsible, stupid, yada, yada, yada. Spare me, okay? She's pregnant and we need your help. Are you in or not?"

I looked at Lena, who was placing the cool cloth on Heather's forehead again, and at John, who continued to stare at me defiantly, and finally at Heather, who seemed to have shrunk into the couch, her pale face a portrait of misery. What a band of sorry misfits we comprised.

"I'm in," I said, "but could you please try not to be so destructive on your visits? My suit, my shoes, my garbage can ..."

"Sorry about all that," John said, his expression changing from defiant to sheepish. "I didn't know she was going to puke. I mean, she's been puking all week, but I didn't know she'd do it right *then*."

"And we still have to call Mrs. Stein."

"I know," he said. "I just wanted to tell you first, to make sure you weren't going to quit when you found out. I'm guessing this makes it harder, right?"

Life without a safety net; I remembered the feeling all too well. "It doesn't make the case harder for me, but it's not me I'm worried about. I imagine life just got harder for you and Heather in all sorts of ways, but we'll talk about that later. I'm not quitting,

John. You don't need to worry about that. But I might start charging you for clothes."

"Oh, right. Sorry." He reached for his wallet.

"John."

"What?"

"I'm kidding."

"Oh. It's hard to tell with you. You're kind of a smartass."

Another snicker from Lena.

"I'll work on that," I promised.

"No," he said, "it's okay. I don't mind. Not usually. And it probably works pretty well in court."

"Sometimes," I admitted. "But not always so well in other situations." I glanced at Heather, who seemed to have fallen asleep. "Speaking of court, I have to be there this morning, and I'm running late. Judges don't take kindly to that. You and Heather can wait here until I get back, but we'll have to—"

"I know. We'll have to let Mrs. Stein know where I am."

"Exactly."

As it turned out, she already knew, as did the officers who'd been sent to the school to question John only to find an empty desk and a frustrated teacher.

Chapter 10: Brian

JOHN WAS TAKEN into custody on an early summer morning a month after he was first questioned by police. At that point, our relationship became official.

Tennessee Code Title 37-1-134 outlines the provisions for charging a juvenile offender as an adult in the state of Tennessee. Greatly simplified for the layperson, and as I explained to Lena, a child under the age of sixteen may be tried as an adult if:

1. He or she has been charged with first degree murder, second degree murder, rape, robbery, or kidnapping;

2. The child was afforded the appropriate hearing with counsel present and basic rights were protected;

3. The court finds reasonable grounds to believe the child committed the act and the child is not committable to an institution due to a developmental disability or a mental illness;

4. It is in the best interest of the community for the child to be detained.

It's more complicated than that, of course, with numerous sections and subsections, but because I know the district attorney well, I knew that was what John would be looking at when the case went to trial. After consulting at length with Mrs. Stein and other interested parties, we decided to waive John's preliminary hearing and go straight to trial. It was a tough decision. With enough time, I may have been able to have the charges dismissed at the preliminary hearing, but I needed more than thirty days to do it, and as things stood, the prosecutor would have no problem establishing probable cause. I hated to admit it, but the evidence against John was compelling. The more we discussed it, the more we agreed that all going to preliminary would accomplish would be to increase his time in jail by the number of days it took us to go through the process. The outcome would be the same; John would be bound over to the grand jury and we'd end up going to trial, anyway.

Due to his young age and the obvious dangers he would face in the adult penal system, I fought for John to be housed in separate quarters in a juvenile detention facility while awaiting trial. Thankfully, the adult system offered no objection.

While Bill conducted his investigation, I began to formulate our strategy. To my way of thinking, we began with two options.

We could pursue an insanity plea. I could build the case that John's chaotic history and diagnosis of Oppositional Defiant Disorder constituted a mental illness that placed John's behavior—in the moment the murder was committed—within the legal definition of insanity. I had no doubt I could find expert witnesses to support our position, but it would still be an uphill battle. Any sort of defense based on the legal definition of insanity is difficult to pull off, much more so than the general population seems to believe. This is particularly true with a diagnosis such as Oppositional Defiant Disorder. The label itself provides the argument, and the prosecutor would no doubt pounce on that fact. He would hire expert witnesses who would attempt to paint a picture of John as a bratty kid, arguing that oppositional and defiant behavior is no excuse for murder. It was an argument almost guaranteed to sway jurors over the age of forty, jurors who grew up before the age of grade inflation and participation trophies, who view the field of psychology with suspicion at best and scorn at worst.

Our second option was a not guilty plea. Given that John maintained his innocence and I believed him, that was the path we decided to take.

That's where we found ourselves as the days grew hot and long, soybeans burning up in fields of cracked soil and the weatherman apologetic for announcing another week of drought. Here's what I knew:

John had a bad temper. At various times in his short life he'd threatened caseworkers, teachers, foster parents, and other children. He'd been suspended several times over the years for fighting on school grounds. The kid had serious anger management and impulse control problems, and there was ample documentation in both family court and Department of Human Services files to back up that claim.

Faith Irving had allegedly confided to her gentleman friend, a warehouse supervisor named Danny Peterson, that she'd recently grown afraid of John. According to Peterson, John's placement had started out relatively well, with no more than the normal adjustments to be expected when taking in a troubled teen. I don't mean to downplay the situation; *normal adjustments* can be difficult, no doubt. Power struggles are to be expected, and God knows, John never shied from engaging. Still, in the beginning he'd attended school with little fuss, come home on time, even helped with yard work and pet care.

But over the past several months, according to Danny Peterson, John had become increasingly argumentative when Faith enforced house rules. The situation escalated when Heather Renfro came to live with them, to such an extent Faith—Danny asserted—had been afraid John's anger would intensify to the point of him causing her physical harm.

Neighbors on opposite sides of the Irving household had heard raised voices, both male and female, on numerous occasions, most notably in the morning the day of the murder.

Most damning, John's belt, black leather with dual holes and double prongs, had been found cinched around the wrists and ankles of Faith Irving when she was removed from the dumpster. He'd been absent from school, and his whereabouts during that time were unknown.

Mrs. Stein, John's caseworker, had noticed a long red mark along John's left jawline the night of the murder. In the chaos of dealing with police and working to find both John and Heather emergency placements, she had initially neglected to ask John how he'd received the mark. It wasn't noticeable the next morning when she checked on him in his new placement, and John denied any knowledge of it. Regardless, she made a brief note of it in his case file.

Was all of this enough to establish probable cause? The district attorney clearly thought it was. Not surprisingly, I thought given enough time, we could find evidence to dispute that narrative.

I already knew John was going to be of little help in building his defense. He was suspicious, defensive, guarded, and altogether self-defeating. It would be a challenging case, and John would be a difficult client, but not the worst I'd had—on all counts.

Right on cue, I heard the soft creak of the storm door and then Lena's step on the wooden porch. "Brian?"

"Yes?"

"You haven't eaten dinner."

I glanced up. The sun was setting behind a row of apple trees on the west side of the property, painting the sky with brilliant colors and turning the leaves into a dazzling montage of light and shadow. I'd completely lost track of time.

"Seven-thirty," Lena said, anticipating my question. "The mosquitos are ferocious out here. Aren't you being eaten alive?" She swatted at the air around her face, then crossed her arms over her chest, appearing vulnerable, looking like the sad little girl I'd always imagined her to be.

I glanced down to see one particularly big insect latched onto my calf. "Apparently, I am." Gathering folders, glass, and notepad, I reluctantly followed her inside. As I did with all my cases, I was becoming completely immersed in this one. I had enough insight to realize I saw myself in John. The history of foster placements, lack of direction, even his angry acting out all reminded me of my younger self. *Projection*, my old friend Anna would have said. *You're projecting your thoughts, feelings, and experiences onto him. Be careful. He's not you.* Anna was as perceptive in death as she had been in life.

But maintaining a professional detachment regarding my cases had never been my strong suit, and after a quarter of a century in my career field, I knew that wasn't likely to change. I was okay with that.

Part 2: Preparing for Trial

Chapter 11: Attorney Consult

"IT'S ABOUT TIME you showed up."

John sat glaring at me, his hands balled into fists on the table in front of him. I wouldn't have thought it possible, but he looked even skinnier than the last time I'd seen him, which was no more than a week prior. His skin was nearly translucent in the fluorescent lighting. He also needed a haircut; his blond curls all but covered his eyes, though not so much that I couldn't see the angry look he directed at me.

"It's good to see you, too," I said, regarding him from the doorway. "How's this place treating you?"

"Dude, seriously?" He jerked his head to the side, shaking his hair out of his eyes. "How do you think?"

He had a point. It wasn't a bad place, as far as juvenile detention centers went, but it wasn't exactly homey, either. I needed to slow down and remember what it felt like to be John. I took a moment to mentally conjure up my fourteen-year-old self—skinny, scraggly, angry—then removed my suit coat, loosened my tie, unbuttoned my top button, and rolled up my sleeves. Setting my laptop case on the floor, I took a seat in the chair across the table from him.

"How do *I* think?"

John continued to glare at me without answering, his gray eyes cold, metallic with anger and, I suspected, more than a little fear.

"I think it sucks," I continued, scooting my hips forward in the chair, allowing myself an infinitesimal slouch against the back—it wasn't easy; I gave up slouching a long time ago—and placing my hands palms down on the table in front of me. "I think just about everything in your life has to suck right now."

He looked down, breaking eye contact, and drooped back in his chair. "Yeah," he said, his voice wavering. "It's definitely fucked up. Not that it was much to brag about before all"—he gestured to the scuffed beige walls around us—"this shit happened."

"Back in my day," I said, "the food tasted like dirt, the floor was more comfortable than the bed, it was cold all the time, and we were either in class, therapy, or our cells. I hated it, and solitary confinement made it even worse. You still in there?"

John's head snapped up. "No. They put me in general last week, which you'd know if you did your damn job. Did you just say you were here when you were a kid?"

"A few times."

"Why?"

I shrugged, doing my best impression of my fourteen-year-old self. "Let's just say it was the best place for me at the time."

The right side of his mouth raised the slightest bit. "Dude, that's cool. My attorney was in juvie." The quirked lip was apparently a smile.

"Cool that I got out," I said, "and that I decided a life in jail wasn't a very remunerable pursuit."

"What's that mean?"

"It means I wasn't going to make any money at it."

He raised a single brow, a talent I've always envied. "You look like you make a lot of money now."

"Because I'm not in jail. See the connection? Now, let's see what we can do to get *you* out of jail."

He snorted again, a sound with which I was becoming quite familiar.

"*Gesundheit*," I responded.

"What's that— "

"Bless you," I said, "or something similar."

"I didn't—"

"I know. You snorted, something I notice you do often. But as far as I'm aware, there's no polite response to an impolite snort, so *gesundheit*. Now, let's get to work. We have some important stuff to talk about."

"Like what?"

"Like where were you the day Faith Irving was murdered?"

"I already told you. I was walking around downtown."

"Do you have any idea how many cameras there are in that area?"

"No. Do you?"

"A lot. And you aren't on any of them."

"So they didn't see me. But that's where I was."

"I have someone who says she saw you elsewhere."

He sat up with enough force to knock the table against my ribcage. "What? Who? She's a liar."

"I don't think so, John. Those cameras *did* see you. Time to come clean."

Chapter 12: Brian

WHEN BILL FRAZIER first told me where John had been the day of the murder, I was so taken aback I had to ask him to repeat himself.

"I imagine you heard it right the first time," he said, propping a size eleven booted foot on my desk. "He was at Patricia's Pawn Shop. The one over on Poplar. Got picked up by two different cameras on his way there, shows up clear as day on the inside cameras, and the owner IDed him."

"But how did he get there? And what was he doing there?"

"As to your first question, I imagine the answer is by bus. He was first picked up on camera a block from the bus stop. That's something I'm looking into as we speak. As to your second, he was buying a knife. Switchblade. Four-inch blade."

Damn. As of 2013, Tennessee has some of the most lenient knife laws in the country, but still. "They sold him a switchblade?"

"When's the last time you visited Patricia's Pawn, Brian?"

"Never."

"Well if you had, you wouldn't be surprised."

————————————————

"Why were you at the pawn shop, John?"

He shrugged. "I'm poor. That's where poor people go to buy things."

"What did you buy?"

"What difference does it make?"

"You know how Faith Irving was killed."

"So?"

"So the owner says you bought a knife."

"So?"

"You understand the implication here, John. You're a smart kid, but you're being deliberately obtuse."

"I don't know what that means."

"It means you and I both know that you know why this is important."

John said nothing, just watched me with those silver-gray eyes.

"I'll ask you again. Why did you go to the pawn shop that day and buy a knife?"

"Why do you even bother asking me questions if you think you already know all the answers?"

"I know where you were, and I know what you bought. What I'd like to know is why."

"Fuck you!" He exploded out of his chair, startling me and catching the attention of the guard posted outside the door. I stood to signal that everything was fine, but John had other ideas. He picked up his chair and threw it toward me. Not *at* me, mind you, but *toward* me. There is a difference. I have no doubt he could have hit me had he wanted to—we were only five feet apart, after all—but that wasn't his goal. He'd wanted to avoid my questions, which he'd successfully done. He'd also successfully obtained a bloody nose and a sprained wrist when several beefy guards burst through the door and pinned him to the floor to subdue him. I knew he didn't need subduing, and so did he, as evidenced by the look he threw over his shoulder at me as he was propelled through the door.

You can't make me talk, that look said. *See how this works? You can't make me do anything I don't want to do.*

The problem with John's line of thinking was that he was wrong. He was right about *me*; I couldn't make him do anything he didn't want to do, but if he didn't work with me, he'd soon discover many people who could. Judges, juries, prison guards … They could make John do all sorts of things he didn't want to do. They weren't working for John, they were working for justice, and there was no guarantee their idea of justice would match ours.

I was the one trying to work for John, because I believed working for John and working for justice were one and the same. He'd come to me for help; why was he working against me?

As I said to Lena later that evening over a pitcher of iced tea on the back deck, he was hiding something.

"What do you think it is?" she asked, reaching over the table to light a citronella candle beside me.

I pushed the candle away from me. I wasn't convinced they repelled mosquitos, and I was always nauseated by the smell. "Do you have to light these things?"

"Do you have to sit outside?" she countered. "If you have to sit outside, I have to light these things."

"It's where I do my best thinking," I answered.

"Your case would benefit from more time thinking and less time complaining," she said. "I'll be happy to take your candle, but don't come crying to me when you're eaten up by bugs."

"I'll do my best," I said, as she settled in with a candle on each side. "If you're finished, I'd like to get back to your question."

"'Do you have to sit outside?' You've already answered it. It's where you do your best thinking while kindly providing nourishment to thousands of hungry mosquitos."

"Smartass." It was good to see the spirited side of Lena again. She'd always had a biting wit, even in the midst of her trial. I'd assumed back then she'd used dark humor as a coping mechanism, and no doubt she had, but I'd been oddly relieved after her trial to see she'd survived with her penchant for mockery intact. I loved that about her. I often thought our bond had been cemented by our shared affinity for sarcasm. But she'd been down lately. It happened from time to time; she'd disappear into herself—into her memories, I assumed—and while I understood, I was always relieved when she returned.

She laughed, the sound music to my ears. "Okay, seriously, what is the kid hiding? Why do you think he lied? I know you have some thoughts, and I'd love to hear them."

"He obviously thought he needed a knife."

"Brilliant analysis, Brian. That's why you make the big bucks. But let's dig deeper. To kill Faith Irving? Or to protect himself?"

"That would be the question. Rather, questions. Two of many." I rubbed my head, which was beginning to ache. I briefly thought of adding aspirin to my itemized bill of expenses. "Such as, what if they're one and the same?"

She paused, candlelight dancing over her cheeks and casting her eyes in shadow. "Do you believe that?"

"That they're one and the same?" She nodded, and I continued. "Maybe. Something wasn't right in that home."

"I know it looks bad," she said, swatting at a mosquito that seemed to be enduring the cloying scent of citronella just fine, "but maybe this is a good thing. Could this be his alibi? Was he at the pawn shop at the time of the murder?"

"Good question," I said, "and it's hard to answer. He was caught on tape walking in just after two o'clock and seen again walking out at half past two. He spent time in the shop looking at gaming consoles, video games, and—of course—pocket knives. Bill is working to confirm he took the bus to and from and will get back to me with that information, along with transport times. In court we'll argue that John couldn't have murdered his foster mother because we have footage of him at the pawn shop and proof from city transit that he was away from home at the time of the murder. The prosecutor will argue that he could have murdered her afterward, and given the temperature of the body and the state of rigor mortis when it was discovered, it would still fall within the window of time. Remember, her body wasn't discovered until eight o'clock that evening."

"I get the feeling this case has a lot of layers," she said, "and I think we're only on the first one."

"And the more we peel back, the more we'll find," I agreed. "Such as whatever John is hiding. Not just the fact he bought a knife, but something more. I've seen it too many times. Client comes in, says they want my help, then doesn't seem to realize hiding information from me hurts our chances. It's hard to win when I don't know what we're up against."

"It's hard for him, too," she said. "When you've lived a crappy life, you start to think everything is your fault, not just the things you do, but also the things done *to* you. You're ashamed."

He'd had sex with me. I remembered the words Lena had spoken during one of our consults as we'd prepared for her trial. *When I woke up, it was pretty damn obvious he had recently had sex with me.* Not *he raped me while I was passed out*, but *when I woke up* ... I reached for her hand across the table.

"You'll get it from him eventually," she said, giving my hand a squeeze before releasing it to slap at a mosquito on her forearm. "You have those kinds of skills. God, why do these bastards love me so much? The little monsters eat me alive."

"If I recall correctly, the ones that bite are females."

"Bitches," she muttered. "Are you getting bitten at all?"

"Not a one. Maybe they're drawn to the citronella."

"I'm beginning to wonder." She scratched at her arm. "So, what's your plan?"

"Keep giving you my citronella candle?"

"Very funny."

I laughed before turning serious again. "What's my plan? At this point, I'm not quite sure."

"Well," she said, standing and blowing out the candles, "if we want to help this kid, we'd better come up with one."

"That's what I'm working on."

Chapter 13: John

THE BASTARDS DRUGGED ME. I don't know what they shot me with, but it knocked me out for a long time. It was dark when I woke up and found myself in what they called the Quiet Room. It was really just solitary confinement with padding; they'd obviously stolen the name from a psych ward. No one they dragged to it was ever quiet; they spent their time in there yelling and cussing out the staff. Some kicked and banged on the door, and others went flat-out crazy and smeared their own shit everywhere. They didn't put us in the Quiet Room to be quiet; they put us there to keep us from hurting anyone, including ourselves.

The first thing I noticed was that I was thirsty, not a regular kind of thirsty, but the kind of thirsty you'd be if you were lost in the desert for days. My tongue felt three times normal size and was literally stuck to the roof of my mouth.

The next thing I noticed was that my wrist hurt. I tried to raise my arm and realized I couldn't; it was wrapped up and caught in a sling that was looped around the back of my neck. I sat up and struggled to remove the strap. Now that I'd noticed it was there, I felt like it was choking me. Between my big tongue and the noose around my neck, I could barely breathe.

"You awake now, John?" It was Henry, one of the night guards, looking at me through the window set into the door. Henry was a big guy, like one of those V-shaped cartoon superheroes with huge shoulders and arms and a tiny waist and massive thighs. You know how girls always complain about cartoon characters having giant boobs and tiny waists and big butts, and how that makes them feel? How do you think I feel, a scrawny-assed teenaged boy, when I see someone like Superman or Green Lantern or Mr. Incredible or Black Panther? Or even Henry? At least Henry was real, but that only made me feel worse about myself.

Still, even though he looked like a steroid-addicted cartoon character, Henry was pretty cool for the most part. As cool as someone can be while they're keeping you locked in a cage, anyway.

I licked my lips and tried to work up enough spit to answer. "Yeah. Thirsty. Dizzy, too." I rubbed the back of my neck where the strap had been.

"Leave the sling on, my man," said Henry. "You done sprained your wrist, fighting like that. What got into you, boy?"

He waited for me to answer, shaking his head when I didn't. "You keep that up, you'll go back to regular old solitary. You know that, don't you? Is that where you want to be?" That time he didn't wait for an answer, which was fine by me. I didn't have one, and even if I had, it hurt too much to talk. "Get you some water; there's a paper cup full on the floor over there."

Did I mention there was no furniture in the Quiet Room? Not even a blanket to cover up with because they thought we might use it to choke ourselves. I guess some kids probably might have. It's a good thing I wasn't suicidal or I'd have just used the strap from my sling. Or the Ace bandage around my arm. Guess they didn't think about that when they threw me in there. Dumbass bastards.

"Try to go back to sleep," Henry was saying. "You'll feel better when you wake up in the morning."

Back to sleep, as if I'd just been sleeping instead of knocked the hell out. But there was no point in saying anything, so I didn't.

Henry whistled as he moved on to the next room down the line, where I knew a pimple-faced crazy kid named Griffin was probably sitting and rocking, banging his head against the padded wall and humming like he did every night. Griffin more or less lived in the Quiet Room, sometimes naked if they thought he'd try to hurt himself with his clothes.

I'd never talked to him, but I'd seen him restrained and carried several times, and I heard his name on a regular basis. *Your therapist is on his way, Griffin, but is there anything we can do for you? Would journaling help? I can't give you a sharp, but I can give you a crayon. Jesus, this kid needs to be in a mental hospital, not a jail.* Apparently one time he had tried to hurt himself by shoving the crayon all the way up his nose to his brain, so now he couldn't even have those.

I swear I'm not making that up.

At least the ringing in my ears kept me from hearing him, for once.

What got into me, Henry wanted to know. I got busted, is what got into me. Caught in a lie. I'd figured I probably would, sooner or later, but I'd hoped I'd have time to come up with a good story before it happened. Good enough to be believed, anyway, but it's not easy to make up a story to explain why a kid might skip school to buy a switchblade on the very same day his foster mother gets murdered. The obvious answer was because he wanted to hurt someone, maybe even kill someone.

And I did want to, but I also didn't.

Look, I knew what my files all said. They said I was an angry, violent, troubled kid. Right? Well, yeah. I won't deny any of that, but the thing was, I never threw the first lick. That's the truth. I'd been in a lot of fights, but I didn't start any of them. Not physically, anyway. I could be mouthy, for sure—that was all I had—but I wasn't violent unless I wasn't given any other choice. You think I enjoyed getting hit? Hell, no, but I wasn't going to stand there and get hit without hitting back, you can bet your ass on that.

I guess you could say being a poor kid wearing the wrong clothes started fights. Or maybe being the new kid at a big school for the twelfth time in eight years started fights. Or maybe being stupid started fights, even if the only reason you were stupid was because you were never in one place long enough to learn to read or learn long division or learn what the capital of Tennessee was even though you'd lived in Tennessee your whole damn life. Maybe not knowing how to throw a baseball started fights, or not knowing the difference between defense and offense, or not knowing where the three-point line was, even if you'd never had a parent to throw a ball with you or watch a game with you or do anything else with you that didn't involve yelling and hitting and crying. Maybe being small started fights, or having curly hair, or stammering when you're nervous.

If you wanted to say all those things started fights, then I guess you could say I started fights. But I never threw the first lick, and screw anyone who said I did. You think I couldn't have hit Mr. Stone with that chair if that's what I'd wanted to do? I didn't want to hit him, I just wanted him to shut up and leave.

But that day, the day I bought the knife? I'd have thrown the first lick if I'd gotten the chance. I didn't want to, but I needed to. Of course, I hadn't known all that other crap was about to drop at the same time. That screwed everything up.

I wondered what Mr. Stone was doing while I died of thirst sitting alone on the floor of the Quiet Room with a big tongue and a busted wrist and some crazy kid banging his head and humming next door. Probably sipping champagne in some fancy-ass restaurant, eating fish eggs and snails and feeling important even though no matter where I'd been or how poor I was, I was always smart enough to know fish eggs and snails were too nasty to eat and I damn sure wouldn't have paid money to do it. Probably laughing and telling a bunch of other stupid people all about the juvenile delinquent who'd gotten himself arrested for killing his foster mom, even though I knew more than he did and probably always would.

I wondered why I'd even bothered to find him in the first place.

I wondered if Heather was okay.
I wondered if either of us would ever be okay.

Chapter 14: Lena

BRIAN CAME IN from the porch to fix his plate and eat his dinner. Because he'd cooked, I cleaned the kitchen, filling the dishwasher before checking on him one last time. As he ate cold scalloped potatoes and porkchops and flipped through files, I quietly turned off lights and locked doors before heading to my room, changing into pajama pants and a t-shirt and readying myself for bed.

Some days, I love evenings. I can get lost in the colors of the sunset, delight in the smell of honeysuckle and cut grass, and bathe in the caress of warm wind across my skin as the stars fade in and the crickets begin to sing.

That particular evening was not one of those days.

Days like that one, the wind I feel is cold and damp, and instead of hearing crickets, I strain to hear the footsteps of someone coming to hurt me. Instead of honeysuckle and cut grass, I smell rotting fish, my own sweat, and the bitter scent of marijuana. I was old enough by then to know that past experiences never leave you. *Getting closure*, as they call it, doesn't mean you close the door on those old demons. It just means you learn to handle them when they show up, getting a little stronger each time so that eventually they can't swallow you whole.

Loneliness had been one of my demons, and over the years, I'd come to recognize three different kinds. There was the kind you felt when you were literally alone, and the kind you felt when you were surrounded by people but not connected to any of them, and finally, there was the kind where you knew no one would notice if you simply ceased to exist. That's a kind of loneliness that's hard to bear.

I was never alone on that riverbank, but I was always lonely. Sometimes I'd imagine everyone I knew, from my family members to the fried pie lady; to Lenny, the crooked cop; to Willie G., who's now dead; all floating in space. I don't know why that helped me, but it did. Something about making everyone else as lonely as I was, maybe, floating all by themselves in the cold, dark infinity of the universe.

I once told Brian my thoughts about the different kinds of loneliness, relieved when he didn't dismiss me with something empty, something like, "Of course people would notice." I should have realized given his history that he, too, would be familiar with that third kind.

Brian being Brian, he didn't say anything for an uncomfortable amount of time, just sat looking at me, hands clasped, index fingers extended to support his chin. "*Mutterseelenallein*," he finally said. "Utterly and profoundly alone. It's German, meant to describe a loneliness so deep it's as if—literal translation—even your mother's soul has left you." Then he stood, walked over to put his arm around my shoulders, and said, "Just so we're clear, I would notice if you simply ceased to exist."

I practiced the word, felt its shape on my tongue and in my throat. And then, me being me, I ducked away from both his arm and his affectionate reply and said, "I would hope so, since if I weren't here reminding you to come in at night, the mosquitoes would have finished you off years ago."

I may have ducked away, but I didn't forget what he'd said, neither the word nor the declaration that followed.

That particular night, the one on which my past threatened to overtake my present, I set the ceiling fan on low before turning out the light and curling onto my side, away from the door. I felt like crying, but I wouldn't. The demons were working hard to get in, but I was determined to keep them out.

There was a soft knock, and then Brian.

"Hey," he said to me, his voice low and quiet. I didn't turn to look at him, but I knew his silhouette was framed by the light of the hallway, the glow around his curls making him look like one of Bernini's angels. For a short while, First Baptist Church had a cheap replica of one of those statues affixed to the wall behind the choir, but that didn't last long. Daddy led the fight to have it removed and replaced with a plastic-framed life-sized print of Jesus nailed to the cross, blood dripping from his head, wrists, and ankles, head lolled to the side and eyes rolled back. It was a horrific scene that never made sense to me, since as any good Baptist knows—not that I was ever, by any stretch of the imagination, a *good Baptist*—Jesus had risen. I mean … that was the whole point, wasn't it?

Anyway, I'd grown used to seeing Brian framed this way—like Bernini's angel, I mean, not like dead Jesus. "Are you okay?" he asked. "You've been really quiet this evening."

I couldn't answer, because I'd stuffed the end of my pillowcase in my mouth in a sorry attempt to stop my breath because I refused to cry.

I heard his footsteps, then felt the mattress temporarily dip with the added weight. For an instant I froze, expecting to feel the tell-tale sign of his price. But it wasn't there, of course. It never is. There was only the feel of his fingers stroking my hair, pulling it off my face and away from my neck.

"Just so we're clear," he said, his voice quiet, nearly lost in the hushed *swish* of the fan, "I would notice if you simply ceased to exist."

I did, after all, cry, but with Brian's words, the demons had scattered to the wind.

Thank you, I tried to say, but I couldn't make the words come out, although my heart was beating their rhythm. What I could do was grab his hand, clutching it in both of mine, holding it to my heart, hoping he could feel what I wanted to say.

We are the children of sorrow all grown up, Brian and I, scarred and imperfect, but muddling through the best we can, growing stronger every day.

Mutterseelenallein, indeed.

Chapter 15: Attorney Consult

"HOW'S THE WRIST?" I nodded toward the sling that held John's arm loosely against his chest.

"It's okay. Still pretty swollen."

"That wasn't necessary, you know. The chair. You could have asked for a break."

"Would you have given me one?"

Good question. "Probably not," I answered honestly. "I'm trying to help you, John."

"Why?" he asked. "What do you care? You and your fancy friends and fish eggs and champagne."

"Why? You came to me for help, remember? And when you told me you didn't murder Faith, I believed you." Had he just said what I thought I'd heard? "What on earth are you talking about, John? Fish eggs and champagne?"

"You can't help me," he said, briefly covering his eyes with his free hand before slouching even lower against the back of his chair.

"Yes, I can. But in order for me to do that, you're going to have to work with me."

"I can't," he said, his voice cracking partially, I assumed, due to puberty and partially to the emotions he seemed to be working so hard to contain. "I came to you because I wanted you to help me stay out of jail, but you keep asking me questions I can't answer."

"Why can't you answer them? Because you don't know, or because you're afraid?"

He sat perfectly still, head back against the chair, eyes closed. I was beginning to wonder if he'd fallen asleep when he spoke. "Have you ever been in a situation where there was no good way out?"

"Yes," I said. "But it gets better. Trust me on this."

John observed me from slitted eyes but remained silent.

"My childhood wasn't so different from yours," I said.

"Were you ever arrested for murder?"

"No."

"Were you ever afraid of *being* murdered?"

Given our conversation thus far, I wasn't quite as surprised as I might otherwise have been. "No."

"Then your childhood was so different from mine."

"Who are you afraid of, John?" We were getting so close to the truth I could feel it.

"Can I have a break?"

Testing me, then. I blew out a frustrated breath. "Sure," I said, "but eventually we're going to have to talk."

"Send the guard in for me on your way out, okay? I'm locked in here until they come."

"Will do." I stood, buttoning my jacket while taking advantage of his closed eyes to study him. When he spoke, voice full of anger and vocabulary full of profanity, it was easy to forget he was just a kid. A skinny, pale, terrified little kid. "Do you feel safe here, John?"

"Yes." Then, "You're still asking questions. You said I could have a break."

I nodded, even though his eyes remained closed. "So I did. I'll be back soon, but if you need to reach me sooner let someone know."

He remained silent and unmoving. I hated to leave him, but he was right; I'd said he could have a break, and I wouldn't go back on my word. I needed him to trust me.

"For what it's worth," I said, pausing in the doorframe, "fish eggs are nasty as hell, and champagne gives me gas."

His lips twitched. John's version of a smile, or so I told myself.

Chapter 16: Brian

BILL WAS PACING in the lobby when I got back to my office.

"He's been here for over an hour," said Lena. "I told him he could call you, but he said he'd rather talk to you in person. He's two cups of coffee in at this point."

"Three," corrected Bill. "And four cigarettes. Let's go to your office." He didn't wait for me to answer before heading down the hall toward my door.

"You're scaring me, Bill." I unlocked the door and motioned him in, tossing my coat over my chair and taking a seat to face him. "What's going on?"

"Couple of things," he said, walking circles around the room. He placed the butt end of an unlit cigarette between his lips and spoke around it. "I wanted to be the first to tell you. We've got the murder weapon."

"*What?*"

"Preliminary assessment is that it's a match, Brian. Landlord found it, a Mr. Ginnis. Avery Ginnis. Said he's doing some renovations to the house.

Hasn't been able to rent it as is; apparently people get a little freaked out about renting what he calls a murder house. Said he's hoping if he changes it around, people won't think about it as much."

"He found it during renovations?"

Bill nodded, the unlit cigarette bouncing with the motion. "He and an electrician. Apparently, the house wasn't up to code and had to be rewired. Ginnis didn't sound too happy about it, spent more time griping about the cost of the wiring than he did about finding a murder weapon in his house. He was working with the electrician when they found the knife behind a light switch."

"A *light* switch?"

"Someone unscrewed the plate, unwired the switch, pulled out the box, Duct-taped the knife to the inside drywall of the opposite room, then put it all back together again."

"Damn, Bill." I had to admit, that was a pretty impressive hiding place. "Whoever did that knew what they were doing, and it sure as hell wasn't a fourteen-year-old kid."

"Could have been," he argued. "Some kids still know how to turn a screwdriver. But I agree it's not likely. I'm checking out the construction crew and a couple of former renters who have arrest records. Don't think I'll get too far with that, though. A couple of bounced checks, a case of disability fraud, nothing violent, and no indication yet that any of them knew Ms. Irving."

"You've had a busy day," I said. "What about the landlord?"

"Checking him out, too. Lives alone, never married, no kids. Owns a house on the street behind the rental. Previous renters say he has a habit of showing up unannounced to check on things. Bossy as hell, according to the construction workers. I'm working on a timeline for his whereabouts the day of the murder, but so far it checks out. He was with a realtor looking at investment properties most of the afternoon. Anyway, even if he'd been there, he'd have to be pretty slick to have pulled off a murder that particular day. He had a housekeeper who came every Thursday afternoon, which would have made it hard for him to cart a dead body around the premises."

"Have you spoken to the housekeeper?"

"I haven't been able to track her down yet. Ginnis says she quit, just walked out one day and didn't come back."

"Not surprising if he's as bossy as the construction workers say. Does he know where she went?"

"Not a clue. No paperwork, no contract. He met her at a bar, and everything was done under the table. Seems like Ginnis does a lot of his work that way. I'll let you know if something about his alibi doesn't check out, but so far it seems solid."

"I appreciate it. I hate to accuse the guy just because he found something police couldn't find in months of searching, but if we can cast some doubt John's way, we'll be getting somewhere. Where is the knife now?"

"On its way to the TBI Forensic Services Division to be tested for fingerprints, DNA, and blood. According to my source, the blood was evident. Looked like someone had tried to wipe it off, but got in a hurry before it was totally clean. Testing is just to confirm whose it is."

"Excellent. How long will it take to get results?"

"It's hard to say, Brian. You've heard about the rape kit backlog?"

"Sadly, yes." Over twelve thousand untested kits had recently been discovered, stretching back for decades. The TBI was on the taskforce to get them all processed as quickly as possible. While they'd made incredible progress, there were still dozens, if not hundreds, of kits in the lab waiting to be tested. "I'm assuming it could be several weeks?"

"Possibly."

"Months?"

"Maybe a couple."

"We can handle a couple of months. I'll ask for a continuance if I need to. Nice work, Bill."

As always, he ignored my compliment. "Anything new from the kid?"

"I just got back from there. He asked me if I'd ever been afraid of being murdered. He's terrified of someone. My money is on the person who hid that knife."

"That's a bit of a breakthrough, isn't it? What else did he say?"

"Not much. Nothing, really. He asked for a break."

"And you let him have one?" Bill's tone was incredulous.

I shrugged. "I'm trying to gain his trust. It's a slow process."

"Want me to talk to him?"

I inwardly chuckled at the image of big, burly Bill trying to make inroads with John. Bill had certainly done his fair share of interrogations, but I was relatively certain Bill's methods wouldn't be the best approach to use with John. In Bill's mind John was no doubt a suspect—old habits die hard—but in mine he was innocent. "He won't talk to you, Bill. The kid is really good at not talking. I'll get what we need. We just have to be patient."

He grunted. "Patience will only take us so far. That thing work?" He pointed to a large computer monitor bolted to the far wall.

"It does. Why do you ask?"

"How do you start it up? I want you to take a look at this."

He handed me a flash drive and turned his chair to face the monitor while I fired up the appropriate computer and inserted the memory stick.

"What is it?"

"Watch. You'll see."

It took me a few seconds to realize I was seeing video from a bus, the camera aimed down the aisle capturing passengers doing what people do on a bus: reading, sleeping, talking, looking out the window. The date on the corner of the screen read January 17, 2019.

"There's John," said Bill, pointing to a seat on the back right. "See his hat? And he's got on that hoodie he always wears, and those ear things stuck in his ears."

The figure did resemble John, but the quality was so poor it was impossible to be certain. "I'm not sure anyone could prove this is John, Bill. What's the significance? Where does this bus go?"

"It's him. He's on camera boarding at the stop on Poplar, the one just down from the pawn shop. And he was caught on another camera after this was recorded."

"Where?"

"At the corner market next to the bus stop on Faith Irving's street."

"He was headed home?"

"Looks that way."

"What time was this?"

"Three-fifteen in the afternoon."

"Meaning he left the pawn shop and caught a bus—"

"Back to the 'hood."

Damn it. As the prosecution would no doubt argue, that put John in the neighborhood well within the window during which Faith Irving was murdered.

"It gets worse," said Bill.

"Don't tell me. You have video of him hogtying her."

"It's not quite that bad, but fast forward a few frames."

"You're supposed to be on our side," I said, clicking the mouse.

"You asked me to find out where John was. This is where John was. That's far enough." He motioned to the screen.

I clicked to play and sat back to watch. "I see I need to think carefully before giving you an assignment."

A street view, obviously from a home security camera. A school bus drives by, and then I see him. This time, it's evident it's John, walking down the sidewalk and heading in the same direction as the school bus. "What's he carrying?"

"Can't tell, but a knife would be my guess."

"You don't know that."

"You asked. I answered."

"Where is this?"

"Two doors away from Faith Irving's house."

"So there's no denying he's headed—"

"Home, ten minutes after he got off the city bus."

Goddamn it all to hell. "But there's no proof he entered," I said, grasping at straws. "The camera doesn't follow him that far. They can prove he was in the neighborhood, but they can't prove he entered the house. Otherwise, it would have come out in discovery. How long does this tape run?"

"I got the whole twenty-four-hour period."

"See what else you can find. What other traffic is in the neighborhood, if any of it looks suspicious, anyone driving or walking to Faith's house. You know what to look for. If it caught John, it may have also caught our killer. How long will it take you to go through it all?"

"I'm already on it. I need to review security footage from all directions, not just the direction John came from. If I do find something suspicious, I'll have to track it down, run the plates, etcetera. This will take some time, Brian. Maybe longer than you'd like."

"How long?"

"Few weeks at least. Maybe longer."

"Is there someone you can bring on board to help? I'll pay them for their time."

"You go all in, don't you?" He pocketed the ejected flash drive. "If I'm ever in trouble, I want you to be my lawyer."

"Tell me something, Bill. Do you think he did it? Killed Faith Irving?"

He sat forward, hands on knees, peering at me from under thick, wiry brows, and I remembered once again why I'd known he'd be the perfect man for the job. His silence couldn't have lasted longer than five seconds, but under his penetrating gaze, that was just about enough time to make me squirm.

"That's a hard question for me to answer, Brian."

"Go on."

He rubbed a hand over his bald head and sighed. "I spent my entire career searching for the truth," he said. "I didn't go into an investigation with any sort of preconceived idea of guilt or innocence. That's not how it worked. This case," he gestured vaguely toward the stack of folders on my desk, "you're wanting me to pick a side. You're wanting me to find evidence that he's not guilty, but Brian, what if that's not where the evidence takes me? What if the truth isn't what you want it to be?"

I considered the questions carefully. "I want the truth, too, Bill. Even if I don't like it."

He stood, pushing his chair back to its original place. "I've got a buddy who's got the patience of Job. He doesn't mind sitting through hours of tape. Eagle eye, doesn't miss a thing. I'll give him a call."

I walked him outside, watching him light up the still-dangling cigarette and cross the street before I returned to my office and closed the door. He hadn't answered me, I realized. Bill had neatly evaded my question regarding John's guilt or innocence. I wasn't quite sure what to make of that.

Chapter 17: Attorney Consult

"TELL ME ABOUT Danny Peterson."

"I already did. He was Faith's boyfriend."

John was as sullen as ever, slumped into his favorite position, his hair now long enough to hang completely over his eyes. A row of bruises on his bicep looked suspiciously like knuckle marks, but he'd ignored my questions and responded by tugging his sleeve down to cover them. At least the sling was gone, the sprain presumably healed, but the cuffs were back, a consequence of what his chart referred to as his "violent outburst."

"I need more," I said. "What else can you tell me? Think of it as ammunition. He's going to say your foster mother was afraid of you. What can you tell me that will make the judge doubt his word? He's coming out swinging, and we need to hit back hard."

He shook his hair aside and sat up straighter. "What do you know about fighting? I bet you've never won a fight in your life. A real one, I mean. Even when that guy tried to kill you, you had cops to pull him off."

"What guy? Oh." I'd forgotten John knew about my pen-wielding client. "Yes, I did, thank goodness. I'm not really allowed to fight back under those circumstances. I assume by 'real one' you mean a physical fight as opposed to what I do in the courtroom nearly every day of my life."

John's smirk served to answer my question. Bragging to one's client about one's own criminal history breaches all sorts of professional boundaries, but since that was thus far the only method I'd found for getting through to him, I seized the opportunity to build rapport. If we had to bond over our shared juvenile law-breaking behaviors, so be it. Trying on one of John's snorts for size, I said, "My second stint in juvie was for breaking a man's fingers."

"*Gesundheit,*" said John, and it took me a minute to realize he was responding to my snort.

"*Touché.*" I was impressed; the kid wasn't a half-bad smartass, himself.

"Why did you break his fingers?" he asked, his expression part curiosity, part cynicism, and unless I was mistaken, part respect.

I hated that it was my own violence that seemed to spark his respect, but I'd take what I could get. I'd never told anyone what had led to my violent act, and it took a few seconds to sort through my answers before I decided to be honest with him. "I slammed a car door on the fingers of a man who'd been doing his damnedest to separate my pants from my body. He went to the emergency room and I went to juvie, but I went with my goddamned pants on."

"Holy shit, dude." His eyes were huge under the curtain of curls.

"Yeah. Holy shit. Life can suck sometimes, John, but if you stick with it, you can make it work for you."

John cocked his head, observing me for a minute. "If she was afraid of anybody, it was him."

"Him meaning Danny?"

"Yeah."

That would have been nice information to have had all along, but I resisted the urge to say it. At least he was talking now. "Why do you think that?"

"Are you going to tell him what I say?"

"Not directly, no. But if I can use it to help your case, I'll have to use it. I'll look for evidence to support it so I'm on solid ground."

"So, like if I tell you he did something, you'll look for evidence to prove he did it instead of just telling him I said he did it."

"Right."

He released a deep breath. "Okay. Because if I ever do get out of here, he's not going to like that I told you."

"Told me what?"

"That when she broke up with him, he went crazy."

Now we were getting somewhere. "Crazy how? Did you see this?"

"Me and Heather both. They'd been fighting all night. He kept accusing Faith of having an affair with the landlord, and she kept telling him he'd lost his freaking mind. That's what she said. 'You've lost your freaking mind.' Anyway, we tried to stay out of the way, but that was kind of hard to do since we had to stay where she could see us. Which was stupid as hell, because ..."

"Because what?"

"It doesn't matter. Anyway, he started trashing the place, throwing things, kicking over the coffee table, that kind of stuff."

"Then what happened?"

"He finally left and we helped Faith clean everything up. She was crying pretty hard."

"Were the police ever called? A neighbor? Anyone?"

"No, it was just us."

"Was Danny right? Was she having an affair with the landlord?" Good God, that had motive written all over it.

He shook his head once, hard. "Naw. Faith couldn't stand Mr. Ginnis. She came home once and found him digging around in the bathroom cabinets. He said he was making sure she hadn't used any shelf paper because it could leave sticky stuff on the shelves. He was always showing up to check on things, like to see if she'd hung any pictures on nails or to tell her she couldn't put flowerpots on the porch because they'd leave a ring."

"Sounds annoying."

"Yeah. She said if he was that worried about his house, he shouldn't be renting it out. She thought he was just being nosy. He's a racist, too. You should hear the things he used to say about Mrs. Stein."

"I'm sure I'd rather not," I said. "He doesn't sound like a very pleasant person."

"Faith used to say he was meaner than hell because he couldn't get laid."

That struck me as an interesting thing for someone to say, particularly if that someone didn't have intimate knowledge of the topic. "Why did she think that? That he couldn't get laid, I mean. How would she have known the extent of his … ah … sex life?" It was an uncomfortable question to ask a kid, but I needed to hear the answer. Besides, given the condition Heather was in, John was obviously no stranger to sex.

"I don't know." He blew out a breath, clearly uncomfortable, his cheeks flushing red, knee manically bouncing. "That's just what she said to Danny. Can we talk about something else? Like I really want to think about some old pervert's sex life. This has gotten hella weird."

"Fair enough." I added it to the list of things I needed Bill to follow up on. "But if he was so terrible, and Faith disliked him so much, why did Danny think Faith was having an affair with him?" Maybe she *had* been having an affair with him—one that had ended badly—and John just hadn't known about it. Even if she hadn't, Danny's belief that she was still made for a nice motive.

John shrugged. "Danny's just a jealous person. He always thought she was having an affair with somebody."

"Was that the end of it that night? You helped Faith clean up the mess and went to bed?"

"Yeah, pretty much. She'd stopped crying by then. She said she was going to get a restraining order so Danny couldn't come around anymore."

My heartrate jumped up a notch. "Did she get one?"

John furrowed his brow as if trying to remember. "I don't know. I don't think so, because he still came over sometimes. He'd show up, and Faith would tell him to leave."

"Did he listen?"

"Yeah, for the most part. He'd call her a bitch or a whore or something, but he'd get back in his truck and go."

"This is good information, John. This is what I've been needing in order to help you." I added still more notes to the list of things I needed Bill to check into. I was going to have to give him a raise.

"Will this help me at the trial?"

"Absolutely. If we can show that Danny had a history of violence against Faith, that would give them someone else to look at. Someone other than you."

"Would he be arrested?"

"I don't know. That depends on whether or not an investigation is opened and if it is, what they find. Do you think he should he be arrested?"

"How the hell would I know? I'm not a cop."

I looked up from my notes and studied John's face, but aside from his typical scowl, it revealed nothing. "Is this who you're afraid of? Danny?"

He visibly tensed, fists balled up in his lap. "Who said I was afraid of anybody?"

"You asked me if I'd ever been afraid of being murdered. That's a pretty good indication you're afraid of someone."

"I don't remember that. Can I go now?"

By that point I had enough experience dealing with John to know I'd gotten all the information I was going to get that day. I had to let it go and hope the opportunity presented itself another time. "All right," I said, gathering up my notes. "I'd rather finish early than have you throw a chair or something and end up in the Quiet Room."

"Did they have those when you were here?" he asked, surprising me. I'd assumed he was finished talking to me for the day.

"Chairs, or Quiet Rooms?"

"Smartass."

I laughed. "I'll assume you meant Quiet Rooms. No, not back then. We had solitary, just like you do now, but no padded rooms."

"You told me a long time ago you'd gone there. Why?"

"What is this, payback? Now it's your turn to ask me questions? I'm the attorney in this relationship, remember?"

John's lips twitched, a good sign. "Maybe. I kind of like that idea."

"Okay." I sat back and loosened my tie. "We're going *quid pro quo.*"

"What's that mean?"

"Have you never seen *Silence of the Lambs?* It means I'll share information with you in exchange for you sharing information with me."

John nodded slowly, apparently thinking my proposal over. "All right," he agreed, "but I've been sharing information with you for the last hour, so it's your turn now."

Damn, the kid was smart. I sighed, acknowledging defeat.

"Why were you put in solitary?" he repeated, as if I might have forgotten the question.

"Which time?"

"Dang, dog." He looked surprised. "How many times did you go?"

"What are the rules here? How many questions do you get?"

"Well, you asked me about a hundred, so ..."

"Ha! Nice try, but not happening. Why did I get put in solitary?" I thought back to my fourteen-year-old self. Maybe I could use John's questions as teachable moments. "I was an angry kid," I said. "I fought a lot. I didn't know how to express myself any other way. I didn't know how to tell people what I felt, whether I was angry or afraid or lonely. Sometimes I felt as if I would explode if I didn't get rid of the anger, so it came out in ways it shouldn't have. I was a smartass—you're surprised right?" John shook his head. "My mouth used to get me into trouble," I continued. "I used to tell myself I never started fights, I only finished them. But that wasn't really true. There were a lot of times I said things I didn't need to say, in a way I didn't need to say them. I had a lot to learn about communicating and expressing myself in healthy ways."

"I guess you finally learned how, huh?" His tone was neither sarcastic nor angry; it appeared to be a serious question.

"I like to think so. I never could get rid of all the smartassery, though. But I no longer use it to pick fights with people. When I'm in court, I use it to make a point. When I'm not in court, I use it to be funny. Does it work?"

His lips quirked again, the most I'd ever seen him smile in one sitting. "Sometimes," he said. "You can be kind of funny."

"Well, I'm glad you think so." I stood. "Because although I have to leave now, I'll be back tomorrow, and tomorrow it's your turn to answer my questions."

"That's not really fair. You ask a lot more than I do."

"Yeah, but I'm trying to keep your ass out of prison, so that makes it fair."

He laughed. I was on a roll. "Good point," he said with a nod. "Thanks for answering my questions, even though it sounded like something from a social worker's *How to Help an Angry Child* PowerPoint presentation. I'll have to deduct ten points for that. Send the guard in on your way out, okay? I don't want to be stuck in here all afternoon."

I was learning there was no getting one over on the kid. "Well, I've been on the receiving end of that technique a few times, so I guess it stuck. Maybe it'll stick for you, too." I glanced up at a movement outside the window. "There he is now. I'll see you tomorrow. Rest up. I have a lot of questions."

He smiled, a real, full-on, cheek-stretching, teeth-showing smile. If that was what *quid pro quo* did for us, I couldn't complain.

Chapter 18: Brian

"LOOKS LIKE THE kid was telling the truth." Bill slid a paper across the table so I could take a look. We were alone in one of several small meeting rooms contained on the first level of the criminal justice complex. Bill had grabbed me as soon as I'd exited the courtroom. I was exhausted after a long day, but I knew Bill wouldn't have intercepted me unless it was important. I reached for the paper and adjusted my glasses.

"Well, I'll be damned. The D.A. must not know about this, or he'd have told me. He's a stickler for the Brady Rule; he definitely wouldn't want me to have grounds for an appeal. Might not have worked, but I'd have tried."

Bill shrugged. "You know more about that than I do. Dated January tenth, hearing set for January twenty-fifth. Not a restraining order, but an Ex Parte Order of Protection. The order was good for fifteen days, meant to protect Ms. Irving until the hearing on the twenty-fifth."

"So, she was killed before the hearing could take place." I looked up at Bill. "Her body was found in the dumpster on January seventeenth. That's quite a coincidence, isn't it? She petitions for an Order of Protection but is killed before the hearing?"

"It's definitely enough to inject some doubt. They don't grant just anybody an Ex Parte Order. That's only for cases where the petitioner is able to show there's an immediate danger of abuse."

"John said he wasn't sure if she ever filed because Danny still came around. Why wasn't he arrested?"

"Can't arrest someone if no one reports anything wrong."

"Meaning Faith never reported any violations. Maybe she was afraid to?"

"Or—and this is a possibility, Brian—maybe they made up. Happens all the time. Or maybe Danny never approached her after the Ex Parte Order went into effect. All we have is John's statement, but he's a little unreliable, wouldn't you say?"

My heart was pounding, adrenaline flowing as it always did when the puzzle pieces started to fit together. "Possibly, but I don't think it fits. He's definitely guilty of withholding information, but I haven't known him to flat-out lie. We need to know where Danny was on January seventeenth. Any progress on that front?"

"According to Danny, he was at work. Records back that up. But he's the warehouse supervisor for a landscaping company. It wouldn't have been too hard for him to slip out and back in without anyone notic-ing. Lot of hours of tape to get through, but we should be finished within the next few days, next Wednesday at the latest."

"Have you seen anything helpful yet?"

"Not yet. I'll let you know when I have something solid for you."

"I like your use of the word 'when.' Thank you, Bill." Every bit of information Bill brought took us closer to creating reasonable doubt, but we were running out of time. We'd gone from months to weeks to days. Without some sort of evidence exonerating John, the judge wasn't going to let me keep dragging things out.

"Just remember, you owe me a hunting trip when this is over," said Bill. "All expenses paid." He tilted his head toward me, looking at me over the top of his glasses. "I should be out on the lake right now."

"You'd be bored out of your mind if that's all you had to look forward to."

"Maybe," he said, nodding. "But right now, I wouldn't bet on it. Anyway, I'd better get home. It's late, and Patty will start to worry. I'll call you when I know something. In the meantime, keep that kid talking."

Easier said than done.

Chapter 19: Lena

"WAKE UP, Sleeping Beauty, before you fall into your meatloaf." Brian sat tilted sideways in his chair at the kitchen table, napkin in lap, fork in hand, head drooping forward. At the sound of my voice, he jerked awake with a panicked expression before sliding down in his chair and rubbing his eyes.

"I'm sorry, Lena. I'm pooped. This case is kicking my ass."

"Your fourteen-year-old client is kicking your ass."

"That, too." He yawned, running a hand through his hair. "But I think we're making some progress in spite of him."

"Good for you and for him. Is John being more forthcoming?"

He shook his head. "No. Yes. But not enough. Do you know what would happen to a kid like John in an adult prison?"

"I do. I imagine John does, too, and that should tell you something. If he's more afraid to be out of prison than in prison …"

"Good point. The kid must be absolutely terrified. We could save so much time, and save him so much angst, if he'd just talk to me."

"Trust doesn't come easy for kids like John. You know that. Plus, you're a little intimidating in the beginning. Your suits, you know. And your hair. Not to mention your polished nails—"

"Buffed. Buffed nails. How many times do I have to tell you? I have *never* polished my nails."

"—and your big words were annoying."

"Really? Huh. Well, damn, Lena, I wouldn't have worked so hard to save you if I'd known you felt that way." He smiled.

"Sure you would have." I returned his smile. "You can't help it, just like you can't help working yourself half to death for John. I wouldn't be surprised if you're moving him in here any day now." I was only half joking.

He laughed. "I don't think you have to worry about that. If by some miracle I keep him out of prison, he'll probably be sent to a residential treatment facility until he ages out of the system."

"Poor kid. I like him. I don't think he's a bad kid; I just think he hasn't had any home training." I was surprised to hear myself utter those words. My mother had said them often, always with a sniff of derision for whatever mother it was she thought hadn't properly trained her children. The irony was rich where my mother was concerned. Where John was concerned, I had only sympathy.

"Very astute observation. I like that. I may have to borrow it sometime. Maybe during closing arguments. With your permission, of course."

"Permission granted." I pushed my plate aside. "Did you ever want children, Brian?" I'd never asked Brian that question before, but I'd often wondered. I knew a great deal about Brian's young life, his history of abuse and neglect, the various foster homes he'd stayed in. But I knew next to nothing about the years between that time and the day he'd showed up at my cell just before I was hauled in front of the magistrate. Something about him always kept me from asking. I'm not sure why I did then, other than that it was obvious to me he liked the kid, too, in spite of his frustration.

For the longest time he didn't answer, just sat staring down at his hands, rubbing his palms with his thumbs as if he were Lady Macbeth wiping away invisible stains. "Maybe I did once," he finally said, just when I'd decided I'd made a mistake by asking. "A long time ago. But my life was never settled enough to have them when I was younger. By the time it was, I no longer wanted them."

"But you like kids," I said, a little surprised by his answer. "I could tell by watching you interact with John and Heather in your office. Even when you were irritated with them, you were able to connect in a way that many people are unable to do with troubled teens."

He nodded. "I do like them. I've grown quite fond of John. Partly, I'm sure, because I'm narcissistic as hell and he reminds me of me." He gave me a wry smile. "My friends," he said, "Anna and Phillip. You've heard me mention them."

I had. He'd never told me what happened to them, only that they were no longer here. I knew whatever had happened left its mark on him, but he'd never chosen to share it with me and I'd never pushed.

"They spent years trying to have a baby," he said now. "Jeffrey, their first son, died shortly after birth. They later found there was a genetic component. It's … I don't want to get into it all." He waved a hand in front of his face as if pushing the memories away. "It was quite painful for them, as you can imagine. And for me, too, watching them go through it and being of absolutely no help."

"I'm so sorry, Brian."

"They stopped trying after that, but then years later Anna became pregnant again. It"—he paused, still looking down, continuing to rub at his palms—"didn't end well. The baby, Peter, lived, but still … well, it just didn't end well for anyone involved." He looked up at me. "Seeing what they went through … No, after that, I didn't want children."

"I understand." I didn't, but I'd asked too much already. "You're tired," I said, taking in the dark circles under his eyes, the wildness of his hair. He'd lost weight; he always did when he was buried in a case. "And I'm sorry for bringing up bad memories. Go to bed. I'll get this cleaned up and lock up the house. Your plate will be in the refrigerator if you wake up hungry and want to microwave it. Meatloaf is always better the second time around, anyway."

I stood to take his untouched plate and carry it to the counter. Outside the kitchen window the sun was setting, wind kicking fallen leaves across grass that was brittle and browning now that fall had fully arrived. I checked the window lock, knowing it was engaged but unable to stop myself, and then closed the wooden blinds. I'd get out the Halloween decorations soon. We were so far off the road we probably wouldn't get any visitors, but I couldn't resist decorating, anyway. No skeletons and ghosts for me; I was a fan of hay bales and scarecrows, miniature straw brooms with plaid bows tied around the handles, and cornucopias full of every sort of squash I could find: acorn, butternut, calabaza, delicata, kabocha, and, of course, pumpkin.

I had not had these things as a child. My family had not celebrated holidays, at least not beyond doing whatever needed to be done to put on a show for my father's constituents. When my sister Rebecca and I were young—young enough to still believe magic existed, if not for us, at least for other children—we dressed in our Easter best for the sunrise Sunday service before hiding Easter eggs in the church cemetery for friends and schoolmates to find. Halloween, we worked with adult volunteers to clear a wooded path through a couple of acres of Mr. Jerry's farm for the annual Haunted Trail. Thanksgiving, we served food to homeless people—many of whom I later grew to know quite well down in the bottoms—in the basement kitchen of First Baptist Church, scrubbing pots and plates until our fingers shriveled and our fingernails split. We collected toys to give to poor children for Christmas, and we picked up burned cardboard and charred fuses at Turner-Hays park after fireworks on New Year's Eve.

And always, there were the cameras. *Smile, girls, if you know what's good for you. I'm paying a fortune for these damn pictures.* So, we smiled, two pretty little girls in ruffled dresses and patent-leather shoes, lips stretched wide and teeth clenched against the pain of a twisted pinch to the back of our arms.

What beautiful girls, the people always said. *And such hard workers! You and Becky are raising them right, Gene. They'll do you proud one day.* They meant well; they didn't know the goal was unobtainable. I learned early on that I'd never make my father proud, so I set out to do the opposite, instead. I set out to embarrass him. To shame him. To make a mockery of him in front of the very constituents he sought to impress. In that, I'd finally found success.

Decorations, I reminded myself. *But no skeletons.* I had enough skeletons in my closet without adding more. The coming Saturday, I would decorate. I looked forward to it, everything from dragging boxes down from the attic, to blowing off the dust, to arranging and rearranging until I had exactly the look I wanted. Brian wouldn't help me, not when he was in the middle of a case. But that was okay; I enjoyed doing it alone.

Shortly after I'd swallowed my pride and moved in with him, as the days shortened and the air grew crisp, I returned home one Saturday with a small pumpkin. I hadn't planned on buying a pumpkin, but the local grocery store had a beautiful autumn display just inside the front door, and at the sight of it, I'd felt a sense of longing, a bittersweet sadness that filled my throat and stopped me in my tracks. I couldn't explain the feeling then any more than I can now, but I knew, somehow, that it was a bridge between my past life and my present one. That the little girl I used to be needed to be heard, and that the adult woman I now was needed to be the one to listen. I bought the pumpkin.

Brian didn't say anything that evening or the next morning. I wasn't sure he'd even noticed it, small as it was, sitting on the hearth of the stone fireplace. He was distracted and distant, already buried in his next case. He'd made no mention of the upcoming holidays, and neither had I. I knew without asking that holidays held no special meaning for Brian, and I understood. He'd work just as hard on Thanksgiving as he did every other day of the year.

That next cold fall evening I'd taken a hot bath, brewed a cup of tea, and propped myself up in bed with a stack of women's magazines. *Heaven*, I remember thinking. Back then, I didn't know how long I'd stay with Brian. In my mind, it was a break, a gift to allow me time to get something figured out, and once I'd accepted, I relished the comfort, committing it to memory so I could revisit when times got tough again. I stretched against the cool softness of the sheets, wrapping my hands around the warm mug and inhaling the spicy scent of cloves while flipping through magazines. Maybe I'd learn something about waxing or plucking or skin care, subjects that had never earned a spot in my encyclopedia of "must know" survival skills during my life down on the muddy banks of the Mississippi River.

That's where I was, deep into an article about the top ten fat-burning exercises for the belly, when I heard Brian's key in the lock. I'd bent the corner of the page to mark my place, setting the magazine aside and working to untangle myself from sheets and quilt to go tell him there was a plate of food in the refrigerator, when he poked his head in my open door.

"Don't get up," he'd said with a grin. "I'd hate to interrupt such opulence."

I settled back against the pillows again. "Did you know the average face has twenty thousand pores?"

He raised his eyebrows. "I didn't know, and that's why you're good for me, Lena. I learn something new from you every day."

"That's according to L'Oreal Paris," I said. "I don't know how they know. Surely they didn't hire workers to count the pores of random people. Can you imagine? Talk about a poor work experience—ha! Get it? Anyway, just a little bedtime reading. Bath, tea, magazines. It's the perfect combination."

Brian was looking at me with an amused expression, and I was happy to have temporarily erased the exhaustion, partly because I was in no small part the cause of it, nightmares plaguing me on a regular basis back then. "I think I'll do the same," he said. "But probably without the magazines, although please let me know if you learn anything interesting about eradicating ear hair. It's a new challenge that apparently presents after the age of fifty."

"I'll wake you up if I find anything relevant."

"No need for that. It can wait until morning."

"It's just as well," I said. "I doubt there's much advice about that particular problem in a women's magazine. Although you never know. By the way, there's fo—"

"Food in the refrigerator." He winked. "I know, not that you're predictable, because we wouldn't want that. And thank you. I'll pass for now. It'll still be there if I get hungry later."

"Okay. Do you need anything?"

He shook his head. "Nothing a long hot shower and some sleep can't fix. 'Night, Lena. Sleep tight."

It wasn't until the next morning that I'd seen the bags he'd left on the kitchen table. There were half a dozen, filled with every autumn tchotchke imaginable:

brightly colored silk leaves, plastic acorns and nuts, spiced pinecones, miniature haybales. On the placemat in front of my chair, a note: *You don't have to do anything with these if you don't want to. But if you do want to, they're yours. Brian.*

I heard Brian move behind me, bringing me back to the present. "Yeah," he was saying, "I should go to bed. You sure you're okay?"

"Of course." I turned to look at him. "Why wouldn't I be? Other than the fact that I think I just led you into the pit of despair."

"I'm fine," he said, "just tired. And just checking in with you. We haven't seen each other much lately."

"I see you all the time, with your head buried in a file, or your eyes glued to your computer screen, or your thumbs flipping through some kind of boring law book ..."

"Stimulating. Stimulating law book."

"Which explains why you're always falling asleep."

"You got me there." He stood and stretched. "Okay, I'm turning in." He stepped toward the hall, then looked back to me. "Oh, if you think of it, would you remind me to check our surveillance tapes tomorrow? I haven't had a chance to do it the last few days, and we only have enough storage for a week. I don't want to lose anything before it's been checked."

"I can check them. You have enough to do."

"It wouldn't hurt for both of us to check them. One of us might catch something the other misses," he said.

"Anyone in particular you're afraid we might miss? Is there anything you need to tell me?" He'd said he'd ask Bill about Rebecca weeks ago, but he hadn't mentioned her again since that conversation.

"Bill hasn't heard anything from Rebecca," he said, as if reading my mind, "but if you check them by yourself, you'll get caught up in watching Ernie and forget to look for anything else." He tilted his head to the side and smiled, no doubt trying to lighten the mood.

"Your boyish charm doesn't work on me, Brian," I said. "Besides, when you're this tired, your dimples barely show."

"Really?" His cheeks pulled back in an exaggerated grin as he ran his fingers over them. "Well, I'll be damned. I'll have to keep that in mind."

I smacked him with the dish towel before he disappeared down the hallway and I reached out, one last time, to latch the wooden blinds.

Chapter 20: Attorney Consult

"I'LL GO AHEAD and apologize for being in a hurry," I said, tossing my suitcoat over the back of my chair and taking a seat opposite John. "I'm expecting a call any minute telling me a jury has reached a verdict."

"Do you think you won?"

"I think we might have. That's the goal, anyway. Now. When we left off, it was my turn to ask you questions."

"*A* question. I don't know about *questions*." He dragged out the *s* at the end of the word.

"Duly noted," I said. "Let's start with one and see how far we get. Fair?" I rolled up my sleeves and rested my forearms on the table.

He nodded slowly. "Okay. Fair."

"You didn't tell me you'd been home the afternoon of Faith's death."

"Technically, that's not a question."

"Good catch. I'll try that again. Why didn't you tell me you were home the afternoon of Faith's death?"

"You didn't ask me. You asked me where I'd gone when I skipped school."

"And you lied."

"Whatever."

"You're eventually going to have to tell me why you bought a knife."

"I've taken up carving."

I sat back and looked at him. "Really."

"Little wooden animals. Elves. Angels."

"You don't strike me as the type."

He surprised me with a bark of laughter before changing the subject. "How do you know I was home?"

"Cameras, John. They're everywhere. On the bus, the street, people's homes. You were caught on quite a few."

"So what? Mrs. Stein knows I was home. That's where she showed up with the police after … after they found Faith's body."

"'So what' is that this puts you there within the timeframe of the murder."

"Where else was I supposed to go, man? School was out by then, and that's the time I get home. It would have been weird if I hadn't shown up. How was I supposed to know I was walking into a murder scene?"

He had a point. "Did you notice anything strange while you were there?"

"You mean like dead bodies and pools of blood? No."

"I meant more like things out of place, signs of a scuffle, things that someone else might not have realized were important but that you would recognize as different."

He hesitated. "No, I didn't see anything."

"You hesitated."

"Dude, I didn't see anything, okay?"

I didn't believe him, but he'd answered more questions in the past few days than he had in the past few months, so I let it go. I'd come back to it another time. "It's been found," I said, trying a new tack and banking on the shock value.

"What's been found?"

"Your knife." I don't know what I'd expected his reaction to be, but I was dismayed as I watched the blood drain from his face. As much as I believed in John, I found it difficult to understand why, if he was innocent, he had such a visible reaction to my news.

He licked his lips. "Where did they find it?"

"Are you sure you don't already know?" I watched him intently.

He rocked forward slightly in his chair, his head hanging low over his lap.

"John? Talk to me."

"I need to go."

"You need to talk to me. This is serious stuff, and we're running out of time. Tell me what you know."

"I don't know anything." He shook his head forcefully, shaggy strands of hair slapping his cheeks with the motion.

I sat silently and watched him, determined to wait him out unless he pulled another chair-throwing stunt.

"I didn't do it, Brian. I swear it."

He startled me not just with his use of my name, but also with the earnestness with which he spoke it. Up until that point, I couldn't remember John ever addressing me by name, unless muttered accusations of "asshole" and "smartass" counted as names. "Didn't do what, John? Didn't kill Faith, or didn't hide a bloody knife in the wall?"

"Neither." His head jerked up. "In the wall?"

His surprise seemed genuine, so I pressed ahead. "If you didn't do it, do you know who did?"

He drew in a deep breath, his thin shoulders rising briefly. For a minute I thought he might answer, but then he shifted in his seat, straightening his shoulders and scowling. "How the hell would I know that?" he asked, and just as quickly, the moment was gone.

"Your fingerprints, not to mention your DNA, will surely be on the knife, and that's not going to help our case." I watched his eyes grow wide as he registered what I'd said.

"Holy shit, Brian. They'll be all over it because I'd been holding it and looking at it. I played with it all the way home." He started to stand, saw the guard at the window and sat back down. The guard monitored us for a few seconds before moving away. "What do we do?"

"We wait to see who's on that knife. It hadn't been cleaned, or at least not very well. I can only assume the killer was in a hurry. Blood was still on it, so DNA and fingerprints will be, too. Yours. Faith's. Possibly the killer's. You could save us some time if you know who that might be."

"I don't know anything," he repeated, then winced so quickly I nearly missed it. "Blood," he said quietly. "Faith's blood. God, that's awful."

"How did you feel about Faith?"

"What do you mean?"

"The prosecutor is going to try to make the case that you hated her. You resented her rules, particularly when it came to the time you spent with Heather, and that's why you killed her."

"That's bullshit."

"The thing is, it's okay if you hated her. Hating someone doesn't make you a murderer. But if you didn't hate her—if we could show the court that you in fact *liked* Faith—our fight would become a tiny bit easier."

John took his time before answering, picking at the cuticle on his right thumb until it bled. "I didn't hate her," he finally said. "I really liked her in the beginning."

"But in the end?"

He bit at the cuticle, sucking at it before tucking his hands between his thighs as if to stop himself from doing more damage. "I didn't hate her, I just … I don't know. I liked her okay sometimes, but other times she did really stupid things, and it pissed me off."

"Like not letting you be alone with Heather?"

"Yeah, like that, but other stuff, too."

"Like what?"

"I don't know." He pressed his palms against his eyelids. "Can we finish now? I'm tired. It's hard to sleep around here."

"I guess that's enough for today," I ceded. "Do you want me to have Mrs. Stein ask them to give you something to help you sleep?"

He shook his head again, less violently this time. "Naw, I'll be all right. It's just hard to sleep in there, you know? There's this kid. Griffin. He's always moaning and yelling. It keeps me awake."

I stood and walked around the table, stopping behind him and impulsively placing my hands on his shoulders. He stiffened, the bones sharp through the worn fabric of his jumpsuit. I gave a soft squeeze, then tapped on the window and motioned to the guard, who sat bent over a stack of paperwork, presumably documenting the events of the morning.

"When will you be back?" John asked. I was tempted to take the question as a good sign, but the reality was that aside from his caseworker, I was all he had.

"Soon," I said. "Within the next couple of days. We still have a lot of work to do."

"Do you know how Heather is?" he asked, the first time he'd asked me about her in all the months since his arrest.

I set my briefcase back down and sat on the table next to him, scooting back so I could see his face. "Have you asked Mrs. Stein?"

"Yeah, but she doesn't tell me anything. All she says is that Heather is fine, and the pregnancy is going fine, and I shouldn't worry about all that because I have enough to worry about for myself."

"She's right," I said, "but I can see you haven't taken that advice to heart."

"It's possible to worry about two things simultaneously, you know."

"Simultaneously? That's a good word. I'm impressed."

"I can throw in a 'fuck' if it'll make you feel better. I'm not an idiot."

"You are most definitely not an idiot, which rather proves my point." I slid off the table. "Bright minds—"

"God, not that again." He rolled his eyes so hard I was afraid he might lose one somewhere back in his skull.

I laughed. "Okay, I won't say it. And I'll see what I can find out about Heather. But I agree with Mrs. Stein. I'd rather see you focus your energy on the trial instead of worrying about Heather. She has plenty of people, including her doctor, to make sure she and the baby are okay. If anything happens with the baby, Mrs. Stein will let you know. In the meantime, I need your help if we're going to keep you out of prison."

"None of you get it," he said, his tone resigned.

"Get what? Tell me."

He stood and moved toward the door where the guard waited. "I can't talk to you until I know Heather is safe. This shit isn't complicated, Brian." I could nearly feel the despair emanating from him in waves as he passed by me.

"John, I said I'd call Mrs. Stein, and I'll keep my promise. But safe from what? How can either of us make sure she's safe if you won't tell us what she's afraid of?"

"I honestly don't know," he said, "but that's what you're going to have to do."

"You're not being very helpful."

"Yeah?" He tossed his hair back and looked at me with those silver eyes, eyebrows knitted together. For just an instant, I could see the handsome man he might one day become if given half a chance. The sheer weight of my responsibilities threatened to stoop my shoulders. "Well, welcome to the club, my man," he said, "because neither are you."

I watched the guard lead him away, then pulled out my phone. Apparently, I needed to call Mrs. Stein.

Chapter 21: John

I WANTED TO tell him what I knew, but maybe I didn't know anything.

Those were the thoughts keeping me awake that night. Well, that and Griffin. I hadn't totally lied about that. His humming had turned into screaming sometime between dinner and lights out. I wish they could have given that kid something to help him. They had meds for everything, always trying to push them on me, but for some reason, aside from knocking him out they couldn't seem to give Griffin anything that would make him stop the howling. Sometimes I wondered what had happened to Griffin to make him the way he was. Other times, I really didn't want to know. Anytime I thought I had it rough, Griffin reminded me that maybe I didn't have it so bad, after all. And that night, even if he hadn't been screaming, I probably wouldn't have been able to sleep.

In a lot of ways, Mr. Stone was like a grownup me. What I mean is, he'd been through some of the same shit I'd been through, which surprised me. I don't know what I'd been expecting, but I did not see that coming. I didn't know how old he was, but I was pretty sure he wasn't born before 1925, which is when a plaque on one of the walls said this building was built as part of an orphanage. It was crazy to think he might have been in the same building when he was my age. What if he'd been in the very same cell?

I couldn't believe they'd put him in juvie for trying to keep some pervert from grabbing his junk. Maybe he hadn't told them that's what happened. Sometimes, in my experience, anyway, it's better to let people think you're an asshole than it is to let people think you're weak. Or he might have been embarrassed. I probably would have been. One time, when I was little, one of my mom's boyfriends … Never mind. It doesn't matter. Anyway, maybe he was afraid the guy would come after him. If that was the case, I knew how he felt.

He had said that was his second stint in juvie. I wondered how many times he'd gone. I decided to ask him at our next meeting. I thought he'd probably tell me because of that whole *quid pro* whatever thing we had going on.

You can call me an idiot, but I also got the feeling he kind of liked me. He joked with me sometimes when he didn't have to. And he kept coming back even when I was a jerk to him. I thought he could probably keep me out of prison, but then what? I wasn't sure who was paying him, but I knew they weren't paying him to help me after that, and *after that* was what I'd started to worry about.

Mr. Stone was getting closer to what I knew, or what I thought I knew. The thing was, I didn't see much. Not enough to know exactly what happened, just enough to guess. But even that much could probably get me killed as dead as Faith if I started talking.

He'd said my knife was in the wall. I wondered what that meant. The last time I'd seen it, it was spinning around on the floor where I'd dropped it, but when I'd gone back later, it was gone.

I wanted to tell Mr. Stone what I knew, I really did, but I needed to know where Heather was, and it pissed me off that no one would tell me. I was pretty safe locked up where I was, but what if I told Mr. Stone and he told the cops and Heather got hurt? Or even killed? I couldn't live with that.

I didn't know what to do.

Next door, Griffin was finally winding down. Maybe he'd worn himself out, or maybe he'd finally figured out it didn't matter how much he howled, nothing would change and his life would still suck.

Part 3: The Trial Begins

Chapter 22: Trial Transcript

The Court: Let the record show the witness has been sworn in and the jury is present. Mr. Woods is also present with his counsel, and the people are represented by Mr. John McDonald. I'll ask counsel for both sides, is there anything we need to discuss before Mr. Stone begins his cross examination of the witness?

Prosecutor: No, Your Honor.

Defense Attorney: I'm ready, Your Honor.

The Court: You may proceed, Mr. Stone.

Defense Attorney: Dr. Grouse, before we begin, would you please remind the Court of your credentials and job responsibilities?

Dr. Grouse: I am the Crime Laboratory Director for L & M Diagnostics. I obtained my Ph.D. from the University of Tennessee in 1979, and I'm certified by the American Board of Criminalistics as well as by the International Association for Identification. I have many responsibilities, chief among them overseeing our forensic technicians in the crime laboratory. We support the Tennessee Bureau of Investigation in the areas of toxicology, fingerprints, serology, and DNA testing.

Defense Attorney: Thank you, Dr. Grouse. Before we recessed for the weekend, you testified for the prosecution that the knife that killed Faith Irving tested positive for the DNA of three specific individuals, is that correct?

Dr. Grouse: That is correct.

Defense Attorney: Would you remind us who those individuals were?

Dr. Grouse. Faith Irving, Avery Ginnis, and Johnathan Woods.

Defense Attorney: Was there unidentified DNA also present on the knife?

Dr. Grouse: Yes, but it was unusable.

Defense Attorney: Explain for us what that means, Dr. Grouse.

Dr. Grouse: In certain situations, DNA will degrade. For example, big fluctuations in temperature such as freezing, thawing, and intense heat can cause degradation. If the degradation is extensive enough, no reliable profile can be obtained. This result would not be terribly unusual in the case of an item, such as the knife in this case, that's been stored in and shipped across various climates and environments over multiple years. The knife from which our samples came was manufactured in 2008 in Guangdong Province, China, so degraded samples are not surprising.

Secondary and tertiary transfers can also invalidate results. For example, if Person A touched Person B before handling the knife, DNA from Person B could potentially be present on the knife even though Person B never actually touched it. People touching different items in the pawn shop, items on which hundreds, even thousands of other people may have shed millions of skin cells, could conceivably transfer those skin cells—and that DNA—to the knife once they also touch it. This sort of trace DNA results in a mixture that can be incredibly difficult, if not impossible, to reliably interpret.

Defense Attorney: What makes that sort of scenario so difficult, Dr. Grouse? In layman's terms so we can all follow, if you don't mind.

Dr. Grouse: Well, when we generate a DNA profile, we're looking at about forty segments that vary from person to person. It's these variations that allow us to pinpoint to whom the sample belongs. But when multiple samples mix and overlap, it's not always possible to tease out each profile.

For example, imagine that each person in this courtroom has walked in with 40 alphabet building blocks. No two people are carrying the same blocks in the exact same order; each sequence is different. Then everyone throws all forty of their blocks into the same box. Now it's impossible to see which blocks originally belonged to which person. Some of the blocks may have fallen in such as way as to repeat a profile or even create a completely new profile—possibly even one that doesn't belong to anyone present in the room. At that point, it becomes impossible to say with any certainty which blocks belonged to whom. It's a bit more complicated in the lab than it is in my example, of course, but that should give you an idea.

Defense Attorney: Excellent explanation, Dr. Grouse. Thank you. Following up with your example, would it be possible to say how many unidentifiable DNA samples were left in the box?

Dr. Grouse: In some cases, possibly. But not always, based on the complexity of the mixture.

Defense Attorney: And the knife? Was it possible to say with any certainty how many unidentifiable DNA samples were left on the knife?

Dr. Grouse: Not with any certainty, no.

Defense Attorney: Is it fair to say multiple individuals in addition to Ms. Irving, Mr. Ginnis, and Mr. Woods had contact with the knife either directly or through secondary or tertiary DNA transfer?

Dr. Grouse: That's fair to say, yes.

Defense Attorney: Are you able to definitively identify the perpetrator from the DNA matches you found?

Dr. Grouse: No, of course not. All we can say with certainty is that there is less than a one in one billion chance that the three profiles we were able to obtain belong to someone other than the three individuals identified.

Defense Attorney: Thank you, Dr. Grouse. Now, if Mr. Woods bought the knife and handled it without gloves for an hour—turning it over in his hands, for example, or opening and closing the blade—would you expect to find his DNA on it?

Dr. Grouse: I would expect to, yes. Humans shed hundreds of thousands of skin cells per day, leaving them behind on everything we touch. Trace amounts of DNA can be found in samples with a few as seven or eight cells.

Defense Attorney: The presence of his DNA alone would not be an indication he committed a crime?

Dr. Grouse: The presence of his DNA on a knife that he physically manipulated without gloves for an hour would not in and of itself indicate he committed a crime, no.

Defense Attorney: You testified for the prosecution that your forensic technicians also recovered DNA from a belt belonging to the defendant, is that correct?

Dr. Grouse: Yes, that's right.

Defense Attorney: Remind the Court whose DNA that was, Dr. Grouse.

Dr. Grouse: The DNA found on the belt belonged to Faith Irving, Danny Peterson, and John Woods.

Defense Attorney: I'll ask you the same question I asked regarding the knife: Since the belt belonged to Mr. Woods and he handled it without gloves, would you expect to find traces of his DNA on that belt?

Dr. Grouse: I would.

Defense Attorney: Would the presence of that DNA be an indication that he committed a crime with that belt?

Dr. Grouse: The presence of his DNA on a belt he owned would not in and of itself indicate he committed a crime.

Defense Attorney: You testified for the prosecution that Mr. Woods' fingerprints were also found on both the knife and the belt. Is that correct?

Dr. Grouse: Yes.

Defense Attorney: Since the knife and the belt both belonged to Mr. Woods and he handled them without gloves, would you expect to find his fingerprints on those items?

Dr. Grouse: Yes, of course.

Defense Attorney: Would the presence of his finger—

Dr. Grouse: —and the presence of his fingerprints on items he owned would not in and of itself indicate he committed a crime.

Defense Attorney: You're a step ahead of me, Dr. Grouse, but I appreciate it. I have no further questions.

Chapter 23: John

SO THE TRIAL HAS started. I asked if I could not go, but Brian said that wasn't an option.

Mrs. Stein bought me some clothes to wear, but Brian told her he wanted to dress me for court, which sounds hella weird, but I'm glad he said it. Mrs. Stein and Lena are nice, but they don't have any style (remember those white tube socks?), or at least if they do, it's old-lady style, which isn't exactly what I'm going for. But Brian has got it going on when it comes to clothes. At least when it comes to dressy clothes. I don't know how he dresses when he's not at work. Probably has dad jeans like other old guys, pulled up to his bellybutton. But his suits kick ass.

For court, he brought me two pairs of pants, one black and one tan. They don't have those pleat things in the front like the ones Mrs. Stein brought me, thank God. And the legs get skinnier as they go down instead of staying the same size all the way down like Mrs. Stein's did. Nobody under the age of, like, a hundred wears pants all loose and floppy around the ankles.

He brought me four shirts in different colors to match the pants. They're long-sleeved dress shirts that button up the front. And he brought ties, too. This is the first time in my life I've worn ties. I have to wait until I get to the courthouse for Brian to tie them for me because they're the real kind, not the kind you clip onto your collar like little kids wear.

He brought what he called a tweed sport coat. I've never had one of those before, either. It's kind of a dark gray color but it has little tan and black threads all through it so it matches both of my pants. Brian said he doesn't want me dressed in a suit because he wants people to remember I'm a kid, but he does want me to look nice and have a jacket for when I need it, although he doesn't want me to wear it when we're in the courtroom unless I'm cold.

He got me a reversible belt with one brown side and one black side, and two pairs of leather shoes, one black and one brown. He even got me socks and underwear, which was a little weird but I needed it so I took it. If I have to have charity underwear, Brian is definitely the one I want to get it from. He brought me boxer briefs in different colors and patterns. That's the first time in my life I've ever been given anything but tighty-whitey underwear from the dollar store. Pretty cool.

Then he wrote a long list about what I should wear with what and how I should put it all together. He has a *lot* of rules about that stuff, like wear the blue shirt with the black pants and the tie that has blue and black squiggles. Wear the black socks and the black shoes and the black belt and don't forget to wear an undershirt. I act like all the rules bother me, but they don't. I wouldn't tell him this, but I've never had dress clothes or anyone to tell me how to wear them. I've always wanted some style, and now I kind of feel like I have some. I have to say, I look pretty dope when I get it all on and fixed right. I wonder what Heather would think.

I thought he would make me cut my hair, but he didn't. He said the curls make me look more boyish, and he wants me to look boyish. Instead of cutting them, he brought some kind of stuff to put on them to make them stay in place so they don't fall in my face. He brought deodorant, too, even though the jail lets me have some when I need it. He likes the kind he brought me because it doesn't just keep you from stinking, it actually smells good.

Lena kind of rolled her eyes while he was tying my tie and combing my hair and making sure I put on deodorant and stuff, but I could tell she didn't really mind. She was just poking fun at Brian because that's what she does. I think it's pretty funny, really.

He has rules about other things, too, like don't laugh during court because it's disrespectful and people might think I'm laughing about Faith, which I would never do, but I guess they don't know that. And don't squirm around and fidget because it'll look like I'm bored and don't care about what happened. I might be bored, but I do care—how could I not care?—so I try to not squirm even though it lasts forever.

He tells me to make eye contact but not to stare. I asked him how I'm supposed to know the difference. Like, should I count to three or something? Lena laughed at that, but Brian said to be myself and feel free to look around, but not to look too hard at people or give them dirty looks. "And don't snort," he said, like I would ever snort in court. I'm a foster kid, but I'm not an idiot. I've seen enough TV shows to know better than that.

Brian tells me who's coming up next, so I know there are some people who will be there that I'll want to stare at. When they show up, I'll take part of Brian's advice and look around like he said, but I won't make eye contact with them because I don't think I can do that without it turning into a dirty look.

Chapter 24: Trial Transcript

Court Clerk: Spell your name for the record, please.

Avery Ginnis: A-v-e-r-y G-i-n-n-i-s.

Court Clerk: Thank you.

The Court: Mr. McDonald, your witness.

Prosecutor: Thank you, Your Honor. Good morning, Mr. Ginnis.

Avery Ginnis: Good morning to you.

Prosecutor: Mr. Ginnis, where were you on the morning of August 12, 2019?

Avery Ginnis: At a house I own at 353 Iris Avenue.

Prosecutor: Why were you there, Mr. Ginnis?

Avery Ginnis: We're remodeling the place after that … after the woman was murdered. Folks won't rent a murder house.

Prosecutor: And when you say "the woman," you mean …

Avery Ginnis: Faith Irving. The woman who rented the house from me and was murdered in it.

Prosecutor: Did you find anything significant that morning, Mr. Ginnis?

Avery Ginnis: Yeah, we did. I was working with an electrician to put in new wiring. I hadn't planned on doing all that, had just planned on opening up the kitchen and living area. Open concept, I believe they call it. Anyway, the inspector came out and said we had to update all the wiring, so I had to call in an electrician. I was helping him, just removing screws and plates and stuff, you know, since I'm not qualified to handle wiring.

Prosecutor: Understood, Mr. Ginnis. Go on.

Avery Ginnis: Anyway, we'd made it to the south wall of the living room where we had to replace some of the wiring behind the light switches. The electrician pulled the box out and I was shining my flashlight in to get a good look around when I saw something shiny. We took a closer look and saw something taped onto the backside of the drywall opposite the switch.

Prosecutor: What did you do, Mr. Ginnis?

Avery Ginnis: Well, at first I wasn't sure what it was, so I reached in and pulled it off the wall. When I got it loose and saw it, I dropped it and called the police.

Prosecutor: Did you have gloves on when you held the knife, Mr. Ginnis?

Avery Ginnis: No, sir. I did not. It was a hot day, pushing a hundred degrees.

Prosecutor: So you held it in your bare hands?

Avery Ginnis: I did.

Prosecutor: Thank you, Mr. Ginnis. How long had Faith Irving rented the house from you?

Avery Ginnis: About three and a half years at the time she was murdered. She signed the first lease in September of 2015.

Prosecutor: And when did the defendant come to live with her?

Avery Ginnis: I don't know the exact date, but it was close to a year before she was killed.

Prosecutor: Did you have any concerns about allowing foster children to move into the home?

Avery Ginnis: Oh, no. No, of course not. Not kids in general, but that one—

Prosecutor: Mr. Ginnis, tell the Court, for the record, who you're pointing at.

Avery Ginnis: That boy. John Woods.

Prosecutor: You were saying you had no concerns about allowing Ms. Irving to provide a home for foster children?

Avery Ginnis: I didn't mind that at all, but that one, John Woods, he was trouble.

Prosecutor: What do you mean by trouble?

Avery Ginnis: Well, I live behind them, see. The house Faith—Ms. Irving—rented from me was my mother's house. Mother passed away back in 2005. It was just the two of us, you know. I don't have any brothers or sisters, and my daddy died in Vietnam. I couldn't bear to get rid of Mother's house; it was all I had left of them. So, I decided to start renting it out. Anyway, my house, the one I live in, is on the street behind it. Hydrangea Street. My mother had been in poor health for a long time, so I stayed close to help her out.

Prosecutor: Very considerate of you, Mr. Ginnis. You were explaining why you thought the boy—John Woods—was trouble?

Avery Ginnis: That's right. Well, it didn't take long after the boy moved in—John—for them to start fighting. I get up early, sometimes before sunrise, and

I could hear them yelling at each other from time to time, Faith and John. And then when the girl moved in, it got even worse.

Prosecutor: What girl, Mr. Ginnis?

Avery Ginnis: Helen, I think. No, Heather. That other foster child. Anyway, after she moved in, I could hear Faith and John yelling at each other all the time. I don't know what it was about, but it seemed like every morning and every night they were going at it about something or another.

Prosecutor: Did you ever say anything about it to Ms. Irving?

Avery Ginnis: Well, not directly. I didn't feel as if I knew her well enough to pry, and they took good care of the house, so it really wasn't my business.

Prosecutor: Thank you, Mr. Ginnis. I have no further questions at this time.

Chapter 25: Brian

"HOW'S IT GOING in there?" Bill fell into step beside me as I strode down the hall looking for an empty room in which to eat my lunch.

For a cranky old man, Avery Ginnis was doing quite well. Several of the older members of the jury smiled as he talked about his mother. Who wouldn't? An elderly man moving close by to help his ailing mother—it was heartwarming, really. Thus far, I hadn't seen a glimpse of the curmudgeon people purported him to be.

"McDonald just had Ginnis on the stand. I'm up next," I answered, finding a room and breathing a sigh of relief. "But he talked himself into a hole, just as I'd hoped he would. Join me?"

"That was my plan. You got food? Patty packed more than I can possibly eat in one meal."

"I've got salami on rye with Swiss cheese, pickles, green peppers, banana peppers, and jalapenos. Lots of mustard, hold the mayo."

"After a lunch like that, you'll be lucky if you can vacate the bathroom in time to get back into the courtroom."

"What are you talking about? This is the absolute best sub on the planet. Delicious."

Bill grimaced. "If you say so. I'll stick to chicken salad and a boiled egg."

"Patty's homemade chicken salad?"

He nodded. "With whole dill pickles on the side." He held one up to show me.

"Looks good."

"It is." He pointed it at me as if it were an extension of his finger. "Eat, Brian. You look like hell. Now, enough small talk. We have things to discuss. Go back to this hole Ginnis talked himself into. Is it the one I'm thinking of?"

I nodded, my mouth full of salami and jalapenos.

"That's a pretty big omission," he said, "considering. Why do you think he did that?"

I swallowed, washing everything down with a swig of bottled water. "Could be because he didn't think it was important. It was a few years ago, after all. Or, it could be because he doesn't want to look suspicious. Or maybe he murdered her. Hard to say."

"More reasonable doubt either way, right?"

"That it is. McDonald is smart, though. He's anticipating my strategy."

"McDonald is a good attorney," said Bill, painstakingly peeling his egg before cutting it in two and popping half into his mouth.

"He is. So far, we've cancelled each other out. John owned the knife so his DNA and prints are on it, and Ginnis found it so his are there, too. But there are potentially dozens of corrupted samples on there that can't be identified."

"We got standards from the pawn shop employees to rule them out, but there wasn't any way to do that for every customer who may have handled it," said Bill.

"Doesn't matter. That still leaves the possibility of someone other than John."

He chuckled. "Probably some dad buying his son his first knife, or an old man who likes to whittle. Maybe a wife buying her husband a birthday present. Someone who'd never think in a million years their mystery prints would be a part of a murder investigation." He paused to take a bite of his sandwich, then sat back and regarded me, a habit no doubt born of his years of interrogation and one that never failed to make me anxious. "One thing I've learned from working so closely with you, Brian—something I've always known, obviously, but never really witnessed in action—is that the defense doesn't need to figure out who did it. They only need to suggest the possibility that someone else did. For me, that's a different way of approaching things. My job for all these years has always been to find who did it."

"That's exactly right," I said, opening a Tupperware container of apple slices and holding it out for him to take one. "Although a part of me would love to know who really committed the crimes my clients didn't commit, as you noted, my job stops when I've provided enough information to create a reasonable doubt."

"Does it ever bother you? The not knowing?"

I paused, apple slice halfway to my mouth, to look at Bill. "Sometimes," I said. "Are you thinking of this case? Or of Lena?"

He looked down, slowly wiping each finger on his napkin. "Lena," he said. "And Rebecca. I can't help but wonder. About Rebecca, I mean. I'd hate to think she did it. I knew the whole family, had for years, since before Lena was born. I worked with their daddy back when he was a beat cop. He was a piece of work, but to think she might have … I don't know. Life can be ugly, can't it? You'd think these things wouldn't bother me by now, not at my age, and not after my career, but they still do. Seems like the older I get, the more they bother me. Maybe because now I have more time to think about them."

I set my apple slice down and observed Bill. He looked the same as always. Bald, slightly overweight, a little gruff. But I'd never heard that tone in his voice before. "This case will end soon, Bill. When it does, I'll see to it that you get that vacation. You've earned it. You and Patty both."

He glanced at the clock. "Oh, don't worry about that." He waved my words away. "I'm just getting a little soft in my old age, I guess. Back to business. Speaking of reasonable doubt, there's a reason I'm here. I've got some news for you."

"The videos?" My pulse quickened at the possibility. "Why didn't you say something sooner?"

"We were talking about Ginnis. But yes, we did find something. Nothing definitive." He held up a hand as if to keep my excitement in check. "Are you sure you have time to hear it? You're due back in court in just a few minutes. We can touch base later if that works better for you."

"Don't play with my emotions, Bill."

We'd been trying for weeks to find something, but thus far, no images of either Danny or his truck had been found in Faith's neighborhood around the estimated time of her murder. The lack of any sort of surprising event or exculpatory evidence was the reason the judge denied my last continuance request while also reminding me that attempting to game the system by intentionally causing delays wouldn't fly under his watch. I'd nearly given up hope on that aspect of Bill's investigation. "What did you find? Did you spot Danny's truck?"

"Not exactly. I mean, not Danny's personal truck, no."

"Then what?" I wrapped the remains of my lunch into a napkin and lobbed it into the garbage can beside the door. Whether it was the peppers or Bill's news affecting my stomach, I didn't know, but my intestines suddenly seemed to be doing an uncomfortably fast rendition of the Tennessee Waltz.

"A truck from the warehouse where Danny works."

"Oh, my God. Are you serious? This is it, Bill! This is what we need!"

"Not so fast, Brian. It's something, but it's not something to get too excited over. First, it was on the street behind Faith's house, Ginnis' street, which is why we didn't catch it sooner. Our attention has been focused on surveying every way into or out of her street. When we didn't find anything there, we started looking farther out. It's a big company, Brian. The biggest in the county. On any given day there are multiple trucks driving down multiple streets all over town."

I appreciated Bill's attempt to curb my enthusiasm, but it wasn't working. "But on that street, right behind Faith's house, on the day of Faith's murder. What are the chances? Where was it going?"

"That's not exactly clear. It was caught heading one direction around two o'clock, and back the way it came around four. Only one camera caught it shortly after it turned in, before it would have made it as far as Ginnis' house, which is directly behind Faith's. That same camera caught it on the way out. It's not a wealthy neighborhood, after all. Not too many people there have any sort of security system."

"But it fits, Bill." I stood and paced, adrenaline pumping. "The timeframe. It fits."

"It does." Bill stood, too, walking over to toss his own garbage into the can on top of my abandoned lunch before turning back to me. "But there's no proof Danny was driving it. They sign in and out, but it's a pretty rudimentary system."

"Meaning what?"

"Meaning they sign in and out on a tablet." He returned to the table and began packing up his leftovers. "Not an electronic tablet, but old school. Paper. When one page is full, they toss it and use the next one."

I could hardly believe what he was saying. "What crappy sort of system is that?"

"You have to remember, this is a landscaping organization we're talking about. They sign in and out so workers know what trucks are available for hauling equipment, dirt, rocks, plants, those sorts of things. They don't have any reason to keep that information long-term." He zipped his lunch bag and stood watching me.

I realized my mouth was hanging open and closed it, swallowing before saying, "But surely Faith's neighbors, someone, maybe even Ginnis, will remember who had landscaping services scheduled for that day."

He shook his head. "No one, which could mean no one had anything scheduled, or could mean no one remembers. It's been awhile, Brian, and that's a transient neighborhood. Lots of rentals, lots of people moving in and out. Could be someone brought some gravel or something in before selling and then moved across the country. There's just no way to know at this point. But reasonable doubt, right?"

I nodded, still pacing, hands on hips, already working out the scenario in my head. "The houses in that neighborhood back up to each other, so Danny parks and cuts through someone else's yard, maybe even Ginnis' yard, to get to Faith's, coming in through the back door." As I played out the scenario, I was hit with a realization so powerful it stopped me in my tracks. "If Danny murdered Faith during that timeframe, John may very well have been there when it happened."

"Might explain why he won't come clean with you."

My mind was spinning. "He might have seen the whole thing."

"He might have even participated in it."

I shook my head. "No. That doesn't fit. John's afraid of someone—afraid of being *murdered* by someone—and this would explain both the who and the why."

Bill slapped me on the back on his way to the door. "You could be right, but so could I. Let me know what the kid has to say about it."

I needed time to sort through this latest information and figure out my best plan of action, but first I had a date with Mr. Ginnis. Thanking Bill and waving goodbye, I straightened my tie and headed for the courtroom, forcing my mind back to the task at hand. The prosecution's witnesses were leaving plenty of openings for me to score some points, and thanks to Bill, my own case was coming together in spite of a client who more often than not seemed to be actively working against himself and a judge who refused to give me the time I needed. Even with everything stacked against us, I was beginning to think we might have a chance.

Chapter 26: Trial Transcript

The Court: All right, we're back on the record. I hope everyone had a good lunch. Let the record show the jury is present. Defendant is present with his counsel, and the people are represented by Mr. McDonald. I'll ask counsel for both sides, is there anything we need to discuss before we proceed?

Prosecutor: No, Your Honor.

Defense Attorney: I'm ready, Your Honor.

The Court: Then Mr. Stone, the witness was previously sworn in and you may begin your cross-examination.

Defense Attorney: Thank you, Your Honor. Good afternoon, Mr. Ginnis.

Avery Ginnis: Afternoon.

Defense Attorney: This morning, you described to the jury how you found the murder weapon taped to the inside drywall behind a light switch, is that correct?

Avery Ginnis: That's correct.

Defense Attorney: You also testified that you met the victim, Faith Irving, in September of 2015 when she saw an ad in the local paper and was interested in renting your house. Is that correct?

Avery Ginnis: It is, but why are you asking me these questions all over again? I already answered all that this morning.

Defense Attorney: Just bear with me, Mr. Ginnis, and thank you for your patience. I promise I have a point I'll eventually get to.

Avery Ginnis: All right.

Defense Attorney: You stated this morning that you hadn't asked Ms. Irving about the fights you heard because you didn't know her well enough to pry. Is that correct?

Avery Ginnis: That's right.

Defense Attorney: How well would you have to know the witness in order to pry, Mr. Ginnis?

Prosecutor: Objection. What kind of question is that? Calls for speculation.

The Court: Sustained. Rephrase the question, Mr. Stone.

Defense Attorney: Isn't it true that you and Faith Irving began dating when she moved into your rental house in 2015?

Avery Ginnis: What has that got to do with anything?

The Court: Answer the question, Mr. Ginnis.

Avery Ginnis: Yeah, we went out. So?

Defense Attorney: In fact, you dated for the entirety of 2016, did you not?

Avery Ginnis: I don't know. That sounds about right.

Defense Attorney: Did you date her at any time after that?

Avery Ginnis: No, I did not. She started dating that big ox, Peterson, or whatever his name is, shortly after we broke up.

Defense Attorney: Were you upset by that, Mr. Ginnis?

Avery Ginnis: That she started dating Peterson? No. Well, I mean, I wasn't happy about it, you know? But Faith … she was … she liked men, and if she was going to be like that, I figured I was better off without her.

Defense Attorney: Interesting choice of words, Mr. Ginnis. I have no further questions, Your Honor.

Chapter 27: Lena

LIFE TAKES SOME crazy twists and turns, doesn't it?
Like me sitting in a courtroom again, which I'd told
myself I'd never do, and watching the man who tried
to put me in prison spar with the man who kept me
out. Tall, lanky, bespectacled, and with thinning hair,
I'd always thought Prosecutor John McDonald
looked more like a college professor than a prosecutor—not that I knew any college professors, having
completed my formal education at the age of 16—but
his mild-mannered appearance was deceiving. The
man could be brutal.

I remembered every word he'd said about me,
from his opening statement (*We will show you that Lena
Reynolds not only had opportunity, she also had motive.*) to
his closing arguments (*She's a sociopath. A prostitute who
turns tricks for drugs. A heartless monster who murdered her
family in cold blood after years of conflict.*).

I hadn't held his words against him, not back
then, and not now, either. He was right that I'd had
opportunity and motive. He was also right that I'd
turned tricks for drugs. The heartless sociopathic

monster part I wasn't sure about, but given the thoughts I had some dark nights, he may very well have been right about that, too. I didn't think so, but it wasn't outside the realm of possibility, certainly not where my parents had been concerned.

All that said, I *did* hold the things he'd said about John against him.

> *We'll take you through the day of the murder, beginning with the defendant lying to his foster mother and skipping school. We'll see him enter the pawn shop and spend nearly half an hour picking out just the right knife for the job. We'll follow him on his walk home, watching as he plays nonchalantly with that very knife, all the while knowing he's going to use it to slit Faith Irving's throat as soon as he steps through her door. Faith Irving, ladies and gentlemen of the jury, the woman who took him in when no one else would, who gave him a home after his own mother had abandoned him. The woman he murdered and then hogtied with his own belt, throwing her body into a dumpster like so much trash.*

I know Mr. McDonald is just doing his job when he makes these speeches, but if he could have seen John that morning before the trial began, standing still as a statue while Brian knotted his tie, waiting patiently while Brian styled his hair, working hard not to smile when Brian held up a mirror … well, there's no way Mr. McDonald could have believed what he was saying. The look on John's face wasn't that of a murderer. It was that of a kid, a young boy who'd never had anyone pay such detailed attention to him, who didn't know quite what to make of it or how to identify what he was feeling.

But I knew what he was feeling. I saw it in the way he leaned in instead of away, in the way his cheeks flushed and his eyes shone. I remember that same feeling on Sunday mornings when my older sister Rebecca would help me dress for church.

She took care with my appearance not because she wanted to, but because she had to. We were expected to present a pretty picture, and it was Rebecca's job to make sure that happened. Don't get me wrong; Rebecca's touch was rough, not at all like Brian's. I'd always gained a few bruises and lost a few hairs before we made it out the door, but when your skin is starved, when your entire body aches to be touched, even a rough touch is better than none.

It wasn't until Brian had finished his brushing and tucking and adjusting that I realized I knew what *he* was feeling, too. That tenderness, the carefulness with which he adjusted John. That aura of protection. I knew it well. I couldn't take my eyes off the two of them.

"Lena? Are you okay?"

Brian had caught me staring.

I nodded, wiping discretely at a wayward tear that seemed to have found my cheek. Goddamned hormones. "I'm fine. And John, you look very handsome."

John allowed himself a smile then; I honestly don't think he could have stopped it. And I wiped away another tear as Brian put his arm around my shoulders and pulled me in for a hug.

If McDonald could have seen what I saw, he'd know better.

Chapter 28: Trial Transcript

Court Clerk: State your name for the record, please.

Danny Peterson: Daniel Peterson, but just call me Danny. P-e-t-e-r-s-o-n, if you need to know how to spell it.

Court Clerk: Thank you.

Prosecutor: Good morning, Mr. Peterson.

Danny Peterson: Mornin'.

Prosecutor: Do you recognize the defendant, sitting over there?

Danny Peterson: Sure. That's John.

Prosecutor: Can you state his last name, too, please?

Danny Peterson: Woods. John Woods.

Prosecutor: Thank you. How do you know the defendant, Mr. Peterson?

Danny Peterson: He was one of the foster kids my fiancée worked with. He lived in her home.

Prosecutor: When was this, Mr. Peterson? Can you give us dates?

Danny Peterson: Well, he moved in February of last year. I don't remember the exact day, but I'm sure you can find it. He stayed there until he killed her this past January.

Defense Attorney: Objection. Assumes facts not in evidence. Last time I checked, my client was innocent until proven guilty.

The Court: Sustained. The jury should disregard that last remark. Be careful, Mr. Peterson. The defendant's guilt hasn't been established. That's why we're here, after all.

Danny Peterson: Sorry, Judge.

The Court: You may continue, Mr. McDonald.

Prosecutor: Thank you, Your Honor. Mr. Peterson, what was your fiancée's name?

Danny Peterson: Faith. It was Faith Irving. She was a beautiful woman inside and out. I miss her so much. It's hard to keep going without her. She was the love of my life.

Prosecutor: Yes, I'm sure she was, Mr. Peterson. I'm very sorry for your loss.

Danny Peterson: Thank you, sir.

Prosecutor: During the time the defendant lived with Ms. Irving, did you ever see them argue?

Danny Peterson: Oh, yeah. All the time. Especially after that girl moved in.

Prosecutor: Were the arguments about anything specific?

Danny Peterson: Yeah. She didn't want any hanky-panky going on. She walked in on John and that girl making out once, so she told them they couldn't be alone together. John didn't like that, so they fought about it. Looks like he didn't listen, seeing as how the girl got pregnant.

Defense Attorney: Objection! Your Honor—

The Court: Sustained. Mr. Peterson, just answer the questions as they're asked and refrain from adding extraneous information and opinion.

Danny Peterson: Sorry, Judge. Didn't mean to offend anyone.

The Court: Mr. McDonald, continue please.

Prosecutor: Did you ever hear the defendant threaten Ms. Irving?

Danny Peterson: Well, he'd tell her she sucked. That was his word. He'd yell at her and say, "You suck. I can't believe they let you have foster kids." And he'd call her stupid.

Prosecutor: Did Ms. Irving ever indicate to you that she was afraid of the defendant?

Danny Peterson: Yeah, she did. He's just a kid, but he's got a temper on him. He'd yell and cuss, throw things, slam doors, that kind of thing. She said she was afraid it was only a matter of time before he came after her. And now she's dead, so it looks like she was right.

Defense Attorney: Objection! For the love of God—

The Court: Sustained. No need to bother God, Mr. Stone. I'm perfectly capable of running my own courtroom. The Court will take a ten-minute recess while Mr. McDonald instructs his client on courtroom etiquette. I trust you'll do a thorough job of that, Mr. McDonald. I can assure you that you won't like it if I have to step in. Don't make me have to do that.

Chapter 29: John

I COULD TELL Brian was mad. He didn't say anything to me about it, but I could tell by the way he
looked. His jaw muscles were clenched and his lips
were pressed tight. His eyes looked different, too. I
don't know how to explain it, exactly, but they usually
looked friendly, like he could laugh at any minute, but
at the end of Danny Peterson's testimony they looked
hard and dark.

He said something to Lena, who was sitting behind us. I couldn't hear what he said, but his voice
sounded angry. Lena nodded and patted him on the
back like he was a big kid and she was trying to make
him feel better. Then she winked at me. I know Brian
told me not to laugh in court, but technically we were
on break, and I couldn't help grinning back at her because it felt like we were sharing a secret joke about
Brian, not in a bad way, just in a funny way.

Lena's cool like that. I don't exactly know the
story between the two of them, but I don't think she's
his girlfriend. Maybe she's his sister, but if she is, they

don't look anything alike. He's tall, and she's short, and he has sort of blondish-gray hair while hers is dark. Either way, she's cool, kind of like a foster mom, but not a bossy one.

Brian leaned over to ask me if I needed anything, and although he still looked mad, his voice was normal when he spoke to me, like he wanted to make sure I didn't think he was mad at *me*. I asked for some water, not because I wanted it but because I needed something to hold onto. I needed to do something with my hands so they wouldn't just lay there against my pant legs and sweat. He nodded and left to go get my water, and I sat there alone except for the guards against the wall who I didn't think would let me get up for anything even if I'd had anywhere to go.

Even though Brian was angry, a part of me felt happy about it. From what I could tell, he was angry at Mr. Peterson because Mr. Peterson kept accusing me of <u>killing</u> Faith. I'd never had anyone take up for me like that before. I mean, I'm not an idiot; I knew Brian was just doing his job. But it was still pretty awesome to have someone like him defend me. I mean, not just defend me, but actually get *mad*.

Yeah, pretty awesome. I kept thinking if I hadn't been on trial for murder, Brian and Lena would have been cool people to know. But if I hadn't been on trial for murder, I probably never would have gone to find him, which is weird to think about.

Brian came back and handed me my water, putting his hand on my head and rubbing my hair around, then pushing it back in place again before he sat down. He didn't look angry anymore. In fact, he was smiling. "Now it's my turn," he said, and he wiggled his eyebrows at me. I wasn't sure what that meant, but then we had to stand up again because the door opened and the judge walked in, so I didn't get a chance to ask.

Chapter 30: Trial Transcript

The Court: Mr. Stone, I trust you're ready for cross?

Defense Attorney: With bells on, Your Honor.

The Court: If I hear a bell, I'll hold you in contempt. Otherwise, please proceed.

Defense Attorney: Thank you, Your Honor. Good afternoon, Mr. Peterson.

Danny Peterson: Afternoon.

Defense Attorney: You testified earlier today that Faith Irving was your fiancée. Is that correct?

Prosecutor: Objection. How is this relevant?

Defense Attorney: For Pete's sake, give me a second, McDonald. I'm getting to that.

The Court: Please do, Mr. Stone, and leave the schoolyard theatrics outside. If memory serves, Mr. McDonald, you opened this door. Proceed, Mr. Stone.

Defense Attorney: Thank you, Your Honor, and my apologies to the Court. Mr. Peterson, when did you and Faith Irving begin dating?

Danny Peterson: In the spring of 2017.

Defense Attorney: And she was your fiancée at the time of her death?

Danny Peterson: That's right. We got engaged that summer. I knew right away she was the one for me.

Defense Attorney: In fact, didn't you and Ms. Irving break up in January of 2019?

Danny Peterson: What? Naw. We may have fought a time or two, but we didn't break up.

Defense Attorney: Are you sure about that?

Danny Peterson: Yeah, I'm sure.

Defense Attorney: Mr. Peterson, I'm showing you a document that's been marked as Defendant's Exhibit D for Identification. Do you recognize this document?

Danny Peterson: Yeah, but that don't mean—

Defense Attorney: What is this document, Mr. Peterson?

Danny Peterson: It's that damn paper she filed for, an Order of Protection or whatever, that paper they served me with, but—

Defense Attorney: Who filed for, Mr. Peterson?

Danny Peterson: Faith, but look, now, that was a mistake—

Defense Attorney: To protect her from whom, Mr. Peterson?

Danny Peterson: Well, she said from me, but that's bul—

Defense Attorney: What is the date on the Ex Parte Order of Protection?

Danny Peterson: January tenth of 2019. But listen—

Defense Attorney: The Ex Parte Order of Protection ordered you to have no contact with Ms. Irving until a hearing could take place and the Court could decide if an Order of Protection should be granted. Your court date was set for January twenty-fifth, correct?

Danny Peterson: I don't know. I don't remember. If you say it was, I reckon it was.

Defense Attorney: What is the hearing date listed on the Ex Parte Order, Mr. Peterson?

Danny Peterson: Let me see. All right. It says January twenty-fifth, 2019. Are you happy now?

Defense Attorney: I am. Thank you, Mr. Peterson. Your Honor, we'd ask that Defendant's Exhibit D for Identification be entered as Defendant's #3.

The Court: Any objections, Mr. McDonald?

Prosecutor: No, Your Honor.

The Court: Defendant's Exhibit D will be entered as Defendant's #3.

Defense Attorney: I'll ask you again, Mr. Peterson. Was Ms. Irving your fiancée?

Danny Peterson: I mean, not in a formal kind of way. I hadn't given her a ring or nothing, but we had talked about getting married. And now … now she's gone. Can I get a tissue or something? Thank you. Excuse me, Your Honor.

Defense Attorney: Isn't it true, Mr. Peterson, that not only had you and Ms. Irving broken up, but that you were the one she was afraid of?

Prosecutor: Objection. Calls for speculation. The witness can't know how Ms. Irving felt.

The Court: Sustained. Rephrase, Mr. Stone.

Defense Attorney: Isn't it true, Mr. Peterson, that she obtained the Ex Parte Order the day after she broke up with you because you had kicked over a coffee table, punched a hole in her wall, and smashed a stack of plates?

Danny Peterson: Who told you that? Look, I was stupid. I thought she was cheating on me with that old man, the landlord. She'd dated him before and I … I don't know … I was jealous. I got mad, but I never would have hurt—

Defense Attorney: Is that what the order says, Mr. Peterson?

Danny Peterson: Yeah, but—

Defense Attorney: Is your position that the order is wrong?

Prosecutor: Objection! This is completely out of bounds. Not only is my witness not the one on trial, but he never had the opportunity to attend a hearing and speak on his own behalf.

The Court: Sustained. Gentlemen, approach the bench.

[sidebar]

The Court: Phrase your questions carefully, Counselor. You know how to do this.

Defense Attorney: Mr. Peterson, once you were served the Ex Parte Order, was it explained to you that you could have no contact with Ms. Irving?

Danny Peterson: [unintelligible]

Defense Attorney: You'll have to speak up, Mr. Peterson.

Danny Peterson: Yeah. So?

Defense Attorney: Isn't it true that irrespective of the order, you continued to visit her at her home?

Danny Peterson: Says who?

Defense Attorney: Just answer the question, Mr. Peterson.

Danny Peterson: You don't have no proof of that. You can't trust nothing that kid, John, says, if he's the one telling you that.

The Court: Answer the question, please, Mr. Peterson.

Danny Peterson: [unintelligible]

Defense Attorney: What's that, Mr. Peterson? You need to speak up so the Court can hear you.

Danny Peterson: I don't remember.

Defense Attorney: No further questions, Your Honor, but I would ask the Court not to release the witness. I plan to recall Mr. Peterson for direct examination in the future.

The Court: Request granted. Mr. Peterson, you will make yourself available should the defense come calling. Understood?

Danny Peterson: Yes, sir.

The Court: All right, then. We'll adjourn for the day, and I'll see all of your bright, shiny faces back here at promptly nine o'clock tomorrow morning.

Chapter 31: Brian

"THIS IS BRIAN STONE."

"Mr. Stone, this is Kathy Stein. How are you this evening?"

"Good, Mrs. Stein. How are you?" I'd seen her at the courthouse earlier in the day, so I was surprised by her call.

She chuckled. "Well, you know. Busy as always. But I'm sure you know how that is. I had a feeling I'd catch you before you left for the day."

"We both seem to be burning the midnight oil these days. I was just about to pack up for the evening and try to go visit with John before it's too late. I have a few things I need to discuss with him. What can I do for you?" I switched my phone to my other ear and grabbed my pen in case I needed to take notes.

"It's Heather. Or at least that's where it begins."

"Heather Renfro?"

"One and the same. She had her baby this afternoon. A boy."

A part of me had known she was due, of course, but I'd been so focused on the case, I hadn't realized it was imminent. "Are mom and baby okay?"

"It was a relatively easy birth, as far as teen moms go. She's young, which is always a risk factor, but she'll be okay. The baby is slightly jaundiced but is being treated with phototherapy. Both are doing well this evening."

My mind immediately went to John. "Does John know yet?"

"Not yet; I'm on my way to see him. But we've run into a problem. In the long run, it's a good problem to have, but John might not initially agree."

"What sort of problem?"

"John can't be the father."

"Oh. But … wow. Okay." So many questions entered my mind I had difficulty knowing which to ask first. For some reason, my brain settled on, "What?" although I knew perfectly well what she'd said.

"You seem to be having the same reaction I had. But it's true. John is not the father of this baby."

"How do we know this?"

"Heather's blood type is O. John's is A."

"And?"

"And the baby's is B."

I did a quick memory search for any knowledge I may have retained from a basic biology class thirty-plus years prior. "And the baby gets one—what's the word?"

"Allele. It's fresh in my mind, since I just had a ten-minute discussion with the doctor. The baby gets one allele from each parent, meaning the other parent contributed a B. If John were the father, the baby's blood type could be either A or O, but not B."

"How did they find out? Is it standard practice to test blood type for a newborn?" A scene flashed through my mind: a manicured front lawn, a man smashing baby furniture, and me, pulling an older woman against my chest to hold her back from what was happening. *Let him be*, I was telling her. *Let him get it out*. A sense of foreboding washed over me simultaneously raising my heartrate and stealing my breath.

"Not necessarily," said Mrs. Stein, "but it's standard to test blood type for a *jaundiced* newborn. Babies are sometimes born jaundiced if the mother's blood type and the baby's blood type are incompatible, so they tested him."

"But he'll be okay?"

"The doctor seems to think he'll be fine; he just has a little extra bilirubin he needs to get rid of."

The tight feeling I'd had in my chest slowly dissipated. "Are we sure John's type is A?"

"We are. It's in his records. All kinds of tests were done when John was an infant due to the circumstances in which he was found."

"And Heather ... What does Heather say about all this?"

"Heather isn't talking. At all."

"What happens now, Mrs. Stein?" As far as our defense went, this was good news for John. It could cast doubt on the prosecution's theory that John killed Faith Irving because she stood in the way of his relationship with Heather. Clearly, she was having a relationship with someone else, either instead of John or in addition to John. It wouldn't *negate* their theory, but it might water it down. It was also good news for John on a personal level, although he might not initially think so. But John was still a child, and his life was complicated enough without adding a baby to the mix. On the flip side, precisely because John was a child, I had no idea how he would react. Would he feel heartbroken and betrayed? Would he be angry? Had he known all along? His reaction was impossible to predict.

"Now we go talk to John." Mrs. Stein's voice penetrated through my thoughts. "It would be better, of course, if John had a relationship with a therapist he could work all this out with, but since he's chosen to reject all attempts at therapy, it's up to the two of us to break the news."

"Whoa," I said, shoving my chair away from my desk as if that would somehow distance me from what she was saying. "That's way out of my wheel-house. I'm not—"

"I'll pick you up in five minutes. You'd said you were on your way there, anyway, so this works out perfectly."

"—even remotely qualified—" She'd hung up. I had little choice but to lock up the office and stand on the sidewalk to wait for Mrs. Stein, quickly dialing Lena to let her know I'd be even later than planned.

Chapter 32: Lena

WITH BRIAN RETURNING late and a long evening stretching out in front of me, I decided to review the security footage recorded the first half of the week. We kept falling behind, Brian and I, and I knew it worried Brian when a few days slipped by without one of us taking a look.

Truthfully, it worried me, too, although I hadn't had any additional feelings of being watched, not even when I was alone on the property, which, given Brian's workload, was often throughout that fall. Still, if I allowed myself to think of the darkness outside and my relative isolation, it was easy to feel spooked.

I still wasn't convinced my sister was behind the murder of my family, and even if she was, I wasn't convinced she'd come back for me. It had been two years, after all, and no charges had ever been filed against her, Brian's hunch being just that. It would be reckless in the extreme for her to risk her freedom by coming after me. Still, as Brian said, *someone* had killed them, and if it wasn't me, I could still be a potential target. It would be foolish for me to not take that threat seriously, even though aside from some sort of residual anger toward my father, who—as all bullies do—mistreated anyone who wasn't more powerful than he, I couldn't imagine being important enough to anyone for them to wish me dead.

During long evenings when Brian worked late, I would have loved to have a dog, both for the companionship and the security. We had discussed it at one point, debating the pros and cons, but although we both dearly loved animals, in the end we decided it wouldn't be fair to the dog to be left alone so much of the time. A dog couldn't stay inside the long hours we were gone, and neither of us felt right penning a dog outside for hours at a time in summers as hot as ours and winters as cold as ours. Running free wasn't an option; Brian had a lot of land, but it wouldn't take a curious pup long to find the adjoining highway. It wasn't a particularly busy highway, but it would only take one fatal meeting with a car to break our hearts.

I'd learned to keep my mind busy reading, working puzzles, papering the kitchen shelves, playing Sudoku. Quiet activities, ones that wouldn't drown out any outside noises I might need to hear. Television and movies were off limits, as were phone calls, had I had anyone to call.

Having sufficiently frightened myself, I made the rounds once again, checking window and door locks and making sure shutters and curtains were closed. I didn't have a dog for protection, but I did have Brian's Glock, and I belted it around my waist, cinching the holster as tight as it would go. I felt vaguely ridiculous, as if I were doing a poor impression of a swashbuckling Annie Oakley, but I also felt a tiny bit braver with the comforting weight of the pistol situated firmly against my outer thigh.

I served up a bowl of the beef stew I'd slow-cooked in the Crock Pot since morning—an easy meal even I couldn't screw up—set the pot to "warm" in the unlikely event Brian had the energy to eat when he returned home, and made my way down the hallway to the home office. Aside from storing an assortment of supplies, Brian never used his office for work-related activities, preferring either the front porch or the back deck when weather permitted, and the kitchen table when it didn't. Since the installation of the security system, the office had come to be what Brian referred to as command central, with various monitors and unidentifiable—to me, at least—technological gadgets and contraptions.

I settled in, beginning with the cameras surrounding the house, speeding up the tape just enough to allow me to catch anything of import without dying of boredom in the process. I moved through each camera, from the back of the house to each side, and finally to the front porch. The most interesting image captured was a family of raccoons caught enjoying a feast of fallen moths and beetles on the front porch one night when Brian apparently left the light on.

Next, I began to move through recordings from each camera installed around the perimeter of the property. Brian had instructed those cameras to be attached to trees at a height of no fewer than nine feet above the ground. The perimeter cameras were all rotating, wide-angle cameras equipped with infrared night vision. Brian had spared no expense when it came to securing his property.

The cameras on the outskirts of the property were always more interesting to review. A water moccasin was caught slithering up one of the trees by the lake, and half a dozen bats were caught by one of the cameras in the apple grove as they swooped and dove, hopefully diminishing the mosquito population that damn near sucked me dry during the hot summer months. A spider of some sort apparently thought the camera on the old maple tree was a good place to build a web, and I was treated to a slightly sped-up version of her dinner preparations as she spun a web around her hapless prey. Creepy, maybe, but not a threat to me.

I moved on to the camera in the pecan grove, where the squirrels were scampering as usual. It didn't take me long to spot Ernie. He had some sort of fascination with the camera, clambering over and around it, sniffing it while twitching his little whiskers. The scene moved quickly from day to night and back again, squirrels scampering, birds flying, and the occasional insect blocking the lens. Predictable, nonthreatening, initially interesting but slightly boring after hours of the same, all the way up until the previous night, when something larger than an insect seemed to be blocking the pecan grove camera.

I rewound and played the footage back slowly. It was windy; the camera caught branches swaying and leaves blowing. After some time—the timestamp in the bottom right corner said eleven forty-five PM—something, perhaps a leaf-covered limb or nest of some sort, fell onto the camera, snagged on its top, and then partially hung down in front of the lens. The camera jiggled under the weight when whatever it was initially landed, but it quickly steadied. The lens wasn't completely covered; I could still see around the object on the right side, so it didn't appear to my novice eye as if someone had tried to deliberately cover it up.

I certainly wasn't going to go check on it in the dark. I would have needed the ladder in order to reach it and clear it off, and while wrangling an extendable aluminum ladder through and around trees in the dark probably wouldn't have been too difficult for Brian, it was more than I felt up to after a long day at work, even excluding the fear factor. Besides, there were plenty of other cameras on the property; having one partially obscured until Brian could check on it didn't particularly worry me.

I switched off the monitor and stretched, cramped from sitting in place for so long. Turning off the light, I headed to the kitchen where I added my dirty dishes to those already in the dishwasher, then filled the kettle and set it to boil. I wasn't deliberately waiting up for Brian, exactly, but I was always more comfortable crawling into bed when I knew he was just down the hall. I'd put the Glock on my nightstand, change into pajamas, and settle in for a hot cup of herbal tea and a good book. I looked forward to my nightly routine; it soothed me.

Once I checked all the locks again, of course.

Chapter 33: John

SO THEY KNEW. I guess it had to come out eventually; I just hadn't planned on it happening so soon.

I think they thought I was going to be disappointed or hurt or something, like maybe Heather had cheated on me with someone else and they were having to break the news to me. Of course that's what they'd think, because they thought I was in love with Heather and they thought I was the father of her baby. I'd lied about both of those things—I was still a virgin, for chrissakes—but I'd done it to help Heather. I didn't like to lie unless I had to, but sometimes I had to.

I did love Heather, but like a girl best friend, not like a girlfriend. We had a lot of things in common. Just like me, she'd grown up without a dad, but I think maybe it was even worse for her because she didn't even know who hers was.

Her mother hadn't totally given up on her the way my mother did me, but Heather had spent more time in foster care than she had at home. She said her mother was addicted to opioids and no matter how many times she went into treatment, she couldn't quit. Me, personally, I didn't think that was an excuse for letting your kid get taken away, but what did I know? As far as I knew, I'd never had any opioids, and besides, my family being what it was, I didn't really have any room to criticize Heather's. For all I knew, my mother was addicted to opioids, too.

Heather was easy to talk to, and even though we hadn't known each other very long, she was the first real friend I'd ever had. I know that makes me a loser, but it's true. I'd never been in one place long enough to make real friends, but me and Heather, we lived together and went to school together and even hung out together. That's why when she told me she was in trouble, I knew I had to help, so I did, even though it meant I had to lie. A lot. A lot more than I'd planned to, but you do what you have to do. One of my foster mothers used to say that, but I don't remember which one.

I don't know what Brian and Mrs. Stein wanted me to do once they'd told me. They both just sat looking at me, and I could tell they felt sorry for me. I could also tell they were tired. Even Brian looked a little old and wrinkled. I'd never seen him that way before, and I felt kind of bad about it. I guess they thought I might lose it and be heartbroken or angry or something, so they wanted to tell me in person to make sure I was okay. That was a nice thing for them to do, but I couldn't cry or get angry or anything; I'm not good at faking emotions like that. I'm not even good at showing real ones. Sometimes I'm not even sure what emotion I'm feeling.

That was one of those times. I was glad Heather was okay; that was the first thing I felt. It was a relief, especially since no one had told me anything about her since I'd been arrested, no matter how many times I'd asked. I didn't feel much at all about the baby, because … well, it wasn't my baby, and I'm not a big fan of babies, anyway. From what I've seen of them they're kind of nasty. They poop and pee and throw up everywhere, and they cry all the time and have to be held and you basically have no life once you get one. I was glad the baby was okay, I guess, because I'm not a psychopath or anything, but I was a little relieved I wouldn't have to do daddy stuff, whatever the hell daddy stuff is. Like I would know.

Those were the things I was feeling at first, but the longer we all sat there, the more I started to feel scared. Heather and I hadn't talked about what would happen if someone found out I wasn't the father. Come to think of it, we hadn't talked much at all about what would happen after the baby was born. We were so worried about what to do when she found out she was pregnant I guess we didn't really think about much except a) making him stop, and b) getting through it. Sitting there with Brian and Mrs. Stein I realized how stupid that was, but it was a little too late to do anything about it at that point.

They didn't ask me who the real father was. They probably thought I didn't know. Technically, that was true because Heather never said his name; she just called him The Asshole, but I knew who she meant. If they'd asked me, I would have lied again because Heather made me promise I wouldn't tell. We argued about that because I thought we should tell, but The Asshole had said he would kill her if she told, and she believed it. I believed it, too, especially after what happened to Faith. I believed he might kill me, too.

Brian couldn't go ask Heather questions because she wasn't his client, but I knew Mrs. Stein would. Sooner or later, they were going to find out who he was without me or Heather having to say a word or tell another lie, and then The Asshole would go to jail.

And if The Asshole was in jail, Heather would be safe.

I wondered if The Asshole would end up in the same prison I'd go to if I got convicted. Wouldn't that be crazy, if we both ended up in the same place? Holy crap, if that happened, I definitely would not be safe.

I wondered how long it would be before they found out. I wondered if he would be arrested right away. I didn't know how all that stuff worked. Could he get out on bail and still go after Heather? I needed to think. I needed them to leave so I could go back to my room and work it all out.

I waited for them to stop talking and told them I was tired and needed to sleep. Brian patted my shoulder and Mrs. Stein gave me a side hug and tried to make me promise I'd see a therapist if she arranged for one, but I didn't promise because she needed to understand I wasn't going to therapy, not ever, and I wished everyone would stop trying to make me. The fact that she kept bringing it up was really starting to piss me off.

What good was sitting around and talking about things going to do?

My dad never even knew I was born, and my mom was a drunk who didn't want me. She smacked me around, locked me up, and ran off and left me. What else was there to say? I seriously never understood why talking about it all the time was supposed to help. All that would do is make me think about it all the time, and why would I want to do that? I had enough to worry about with what was happening *now* without worrying about what happened to me when I was eight.

Now I was locked up temporarily while waiting to see if I would be locked up forever, and Heather had a baby that wasn't mine and I already knew that. Unless a therapist could tell me how to keep one of us from getting killed—and they couldn't, because 'tell me how that makes you feel' doesn't do shit when you're about to be murdered—everybody needed to just get out of my face and shut the hell up about therapy.

Session *over*.

Chapter 34: Brian

"HOW DID he take it?" Bill had to yell over the sound of gunfire to make himself heard.

We'd spent Saturday morning at the shooting range blowing off steam, as Bill put it. It had been a long, difficult week, with both of us working nonstop. We needed to touch base, but neither of us could stand the thought of meeting at my office. I'd initially considered inviting him to my place to go fishing, but I didn't want him to have to make the long drive, and I didn't want to waste a good fishing trip talking shop.

Bill was the one who came up with the idea of target practice at a range located in a small community at the midpoint between our two homes. We both enjoyed shooting, and target practice was a good balance between our work lives and our home lives, related enough to our work that we wouldn't feel as if we were ruining a fun hobby with shop talk, but still an agreeable way to spend the morning.

We'd held a friendly competition, with Bill coming out the winner, and were headed to our cars to go grab some lunch. "I'd like to answer that question,

Bill," I said, "but I can't. He barely had any reaction at all. Mrs. Stein said Heather was refusing to talk, and it looks like John has fallen in line behind her."

"Meet up at Nell's Café?"

"Sounds good."

I spent the drive to Nell's mulling over Bill's question. Did John know who the father was and choose to keep it to himself? Or did he not even know? Whatever the answer was, the previous night had not been the time to ask. I voiced my thoughts to Bill over a bacon cheeseburger and a platter of onion rings.

"Can we get DNA from the baby?" he asked.

"Mrs. Stein is already checking into it."

"Wouldn't it be interesting if the father's DNA matches what we already have." He spoke it as a statement, not a question.

"Since Ginnis has an alibi, you mean Peterson," I said, matching his tone. "You think Faith was starting to figure things out, so he had to get rid of her." The thought had crossed my mind, as well. "Peterson's DNA and prints were on the belt, but not the knife."

Bill shrugged. "Peterson could have worn gloves the day of the crime. Prints on the belt could have happened previously. As you've pointed out, he was over there all the time. Maybe he picked it up at some point, moved it out of the way, told John to put it in his room. Any of those scenarios would explain why he's on the belt but not the knife."

I nodded, considering Bill's words. "That would certainly be a motive."

We paused as the server refilled our tea. I was grateful for the interruption no matter how brief. I found the topic nearly too repulsive to consider despite the fact it could potentially exonerate John.

"If Peterson is the father, I'll have enough for an acquittal," I said, once the server was out of earshot.

"You think so?"

"I do. Even if it turns out not to be him, we might still have enough to file a motion for judgment of acquittal before submission to the jury. The fact that it isn't John undermines the basis for their entire case."

"How often do those motions work?"

"Virtually never."

"How often has one of yours worked?"

"Never. But it should this time, the operative word being *should*. And if it doesn't, I have a couple of witnesses who will knock it out of the park, you being one of them. I don't want to jinx us, but I just can't see how the jury could possibly return a verdict other than not guilty."

"You sound awfully sure of that."

"Your help has been instrumental, Bill. You've dug so much deeper than the prosecution did. Hell, you've continued digging every damn day throughout the trial. Because of you, we have both the Order of Protection and footage of that truck."

"To be fair," he said, reaching across the table for the bottle of ketchup, "it's a lot harder to track down a suspect than it is to keep looking once he's been arrested. They laid the groundwork. I just picked up where they left off. And they still have a lot of evidence against John, circumstantial or not."

"Granted, but we have plenty that points away from him."

"I'll admit your collection is growing," said Bill. "But enough of this awful stuff. How's Lena doing?"

I was as happy as he was to move on to other topics, but the new one didn't make my burger look any more appetizing than the old one had.

"As far as Lena knows, she's fine," I said, "but that's only because she doesn't know everything."

"What do you mean?"

"She decided to check our surveillance video last night while I was with Mrs. Stein and John."

"And?"

"And when she got to the camera in the pecan grove, she saw something fall onto the camera, then hang over it obscuring part of the view. She thought it was probably a branch or something that fell during the strong winds we were having. It was late, so she decided she'd just tell me about it this morning."

"And? Don't make me keep asking, Brian." He pushed his plate aside to join mine, his appetite having also apparently disappeared.

"And I went out to check this morning, just to see what it was so I'd know what I'm dealing with when I get home today. It wasn't a branch."

"What was it? Don't keep me in suspense."

"It was Ernie."

"What? Who the hell is Ernie?"

"He's a squirrel Lena likes to watch when she checks the cameras. She's named everything. Squirrels, birds, bugs. Ernie was her favorite." I motioned to the server to bring our checks and a couple of to-go boxes. "He was dead. I was confused at first. What did he do, lose his footing and fall? Does that happen with squirrels? But I didn't want her to come out and see him, so I went ahead and got the ladder so I could get him down. He hadn't fallen. It wasn't an accident. He was riddled with pellet holes. Several of the little steel balls—you know the kind, like you use with one of those Daisy BB guns we all had as kids—anyway, several of them fell out of him when I picked him up."

Bill frowned. "Did the cameras catch anything else?"

I shook my head. "Nothing. I guess it's possible we didn't have a specific camera aimed at the specific point of entry. It's a big place; it would be damn near impossible to have every inch covered, but we're about as close as we can get. We have over a dozen cameras out there, Bill."

"It's like someone has been surveilling your surveillance system."

The server appeared with the requested checks and boxes, then wished us a good afternoon before rushing off to a busier table. After a brief power struggle, I managed to snag the bills and pay for both our lunches, leaving a hefty tip for the overworked server. We stood to leave.

"What did you tell Lena?"

"Nothing yet. She was in the shower when I went outside, so she doesn't even know I went out to check. And maybe it had nothing to do with Lena. Maybe it was meant for me. But it's a little strange whoever did it chose the very squirrel Lena dotes on. She talks about that squirrel all the time. Still, I don't want to alarm her if I don't have to."

"Where is she now?" Bill held the door for me as we stepped into the cool autumn afternoon.

"At a basket-weaving class."

"A what?" We'd parked next to each other and now leaned against Bill's truck as we finished the conversation. The restaurant had been uncomfortably warm; the crisp breeze was a refreshing change.

"Basket weaving. You know how she likes to decorate for fall. Corn, squash, haybales, leaves. That sort of thing. She found a class at the community center that teaches how to weave a cornucopia basket. She was excited; she couldn't wait to get there today. She won't be home for another hour or so. I made sure I'd be home before she is."

"What did you do with the pellets?"

"Wrapped them up with Ernie and stashed everything in a box in the garage. When Lena left, I buried him farther out on the property, close to the lake. Lena's terrified of snakes; she rarely goes out that far without me."

"I need them. I'd prefer to get them before the squirrel has decomposed too much. What are your plans tomorrow evening?"

"I'm sure I'll be working on cases at home, but we can't go digging while Lena—"

"You take Lena out for dinner. Celebrate her cornucopia basket or something. Patty has choir practice Sunday evenings; they're already working on the Christmas cantata, so it'll last a couple of hours. While she's there, I'll come dig. I'd like to take a look around while I'm out there, see if I see anything else out of place. I'll be on all the cameras, of course, so make sure you delete that footage before Lena can see it. Better delete the whole weekend, since the last thing you want her to see is you burying her squirrel. Make me a copy of the footage she watched, though. Give me the whole night recorded by that camera. I'd like to go through it myself. Lena could have missed something."

"Bill, I don't know how to thank you for everything."

He waved my thanks away and pushed the button on his key fob, unlocking his truck with a soft beep and opening the door. "Text me when it's safe for me to come."

I stepped back, pulling my own keys from my pocket. "Will do. And thanks again."

He stepped up and into the truck, closing his door with a soft *thud* before cranking the engine to life. Backing out faster than was typical for him, he roared across the parking lot as if Lena's life depended on it.

And maybe it did.

Chapter 35: Trial Transcript

The Court: Mr. McDonald, you may proceed.

Prosecutor: Thank you, Your Honor. Mrs. Maynard, you were neighbors with Ms. Irving, is that correct?

Mrs. Maynard: Yes, sir. I live in the house right next door to her, on the right side if you're facing the houses.

Prosecutor: I'm going to give you this pointer, Mrs. Maynard. Can you point to Ms. Irving's house on the satellite picture here?

Mrs. Maynard: Yes, sir, It's right here.

Prosecutor: And your house is where?

Mrs. Maynard: It's right here, the one with the above-ground pool in back.

Prosecutor: How big is your lot, Mrs. Maynard?

Mrs. Maynard: It's just over a quarter acre. Point twenty-nine. They're all the same size on our street. Maple Grove is an older development, built in the late sixties and early seventies.

Prosecutor: So not a huge yard.

Mrs. Maynard: No sir, not at all.

Prosecutor: Close enough to hear the neighbors?

Mrs. Maynard: Yes, sir, sometimes. If they're yelling, or if the windows are open or they're out in the yard.

Prosecutor: Mrs. Maynard, were you able to hear voices from Mrs. Irving's house on the morning of January seventeenth of this year?

Mrs. Maynard: I was. They were fighting over there.

Prosecutor: What time was this, Mrs. Maynard?

Mrs. Maynard: Oh, it was early. It started just after 7:00 AM. I know, because I was getting my grandson ready for daycare. He stays with me, because his mother … well, that's not important. But I was getting him ready to drop him off at Friendly Panda Daycare so I could go to work.

Prosecutor: What did you hear, Mrs. Maynard?

Mrs. Maynard: Well, I heard Faith arguing with him. I couldn't hear exactly what they were saying, but the tone was very angry.

Prosecutor: You're pointing at the defendant. Can you say his name for the record?

Mrs. Maynard: John Woods. I didn't know his last name back then, but I know it now.

Prosecutor: Thank you Mrs. Maynard. How long did the yelling last?

Mrs. Maynard: Ten minutes or so, until he—I mean, until John—left for school. I heard the door slam and then I saw him walking fast in front of my house toward the school bus stop. He was hitting his palm with his fist, like this. After he left, all the yelling next door stopped.

Prosecutor: Thank you, Mrs. Maynard. Your Honor, I have nothing else.

The Court: Mr. Stone? Your witness.

Defense Attorney: Thank you, Your Honor. Good morning, Mrs. Maynard.

Mrs. Maynard: Good morning.

Defense Attorney: Now, you've testified that the defendant and Ms. Irving were arguing, is that correct?

Mrs. Maynard: Yes.

Defense Attorney: Did you see them arguing?

Mrs. Maynard: No, but I heard them.

Defense Attorney: And you recognized Ms. Irving's voice?

Mrs. Maynard: That's right.

Defense Attorney: Have you ever spoken to my client, Mrs. Maynard?

Mrs. Maynard: No, I don't believe I have.

Defense Attorney: Can you describe his voice?

Mrs. Maynard: I can describe what I heard that morning.

Defense Attorney: How did you know it was my client's voice?

Mrs. Maynard: Who else could it have been?

Defense Attorney: But when the fighting occurred, you couldn't see them?

Mrs. Maynard: No.

Defense Attorney: So you can't say for certain that Ms. Irving was arguing with my client, can you?

Mrs. Maynard: When you put it that way, no, but like I said, who else could it have been?

Defense Attorney: You mentioned that you couldn't hear exactly what they were saying, correct?

Mrs. Maynard: Right. Just that it was angry.

Defense Attorney: Did you hear my client threaten Ms. Irving in any way?

Mrs. Maynard: It sounded threatening.

Defense Attorney: But you didn't hear any threatening words.

Mrs. Maynard: Not that I could make out, no.

Defense Attorney: So your testimony is that Ms. Irving was arguing with someone you didn't see, who was saying things you couldn't hear? Is that correct?

Prosecutor: Objection. He's badgering the witness, Your Honor.

The Court: Sustained. Your questions have been answered, Counselor. Do you have others?

Defense Attorney. No, nothing further, Your Honor. Thank you, Mrs. Maynard.

Chapter 36: Brian

"YOUR CELL IS ringing. It's Bill." I looked up to see Lena, hand outstretched, holding my buzzing phone.

"Ah, damn. There's no rest for the weary. Thanks, Lena. Sorry if it woke you."

"Not at all. I was just about to watch the news before calling it a night. Try not to stay up too late. It's a school night." I gave her a thumbs-up and she stepped back inside, pulling the door closed behind her.

It was just before ten, and I'd retired to the back deck with a whisky glass of Scotch sans ice. I don't drink often, much less on school nights, as Lena called them, but I was hoping a shot of whiskey would make sleep come more easily than it had the past couple of nights. The appearance of Bill's name on my phone screen assured me my goal was not going to be met.

"What can I do for you, Bill? I'd have assumed you'd be in bed by now."

He snorted, sounding eerily like John. "That was the plan, but you know what they say. I've got some news for you, and I wanted to get it to you sooner rather than later. Is Lena with you?"

"No, I'm on the deck. Do you want me to get her?"

"No, I was hoping to talk to you alone. I just finished reviewing all the footage. Nothing noteworthy on it aside from what Lena described, but I found something while I was poking through your yard last night."

Although I'd always felt safe on the property, I was suddenly keenly aware of how isolated we were and how dark it was outside the soft light of the deck. I set my untouched glass aside. "What did you find?"

"Scuff marks on a couple of tree trunks. Looked like someone had climbed up and stayed awhile."

"Someone sat in a tree and watched us?" The hair prickled on the back of my neck, and I shifted my chair to put my back against the wall. The night suddenly seemed darker, quieter than before Bill's call.

"Two trees. Check out the smaller pecan tree, the one hidden slightly behind the tree across from where the squirrel was."

"And the other?" I peered into the night as if I might see the trees, but there was no visible moon, and the light spilling over from the deck only illuminated the first few feet of the planters on either side, Lena's haybales and scarecrows blowing gently in the soft night air.

"Closer to the lake, but with a good pair of binoculars, a person could see directly into your kitchen."

I took a minute to absorb what Bill had said. "Someone has scoped out the surveillance system well enough and long enough to know exactly how to get to those trees without being caught on camera."

"That's how it appears. Or ..."

"Spit it out, Bill."

"Or someone has hacked in."

I could literally feel my blood pressure rise. "You mean someone can turn our cameras off and on at will."

"I think it's something we need to consider. I'm assuming when you and Lena watch footage from all the cameras you speed it up or fast-forward through sections."

"We speed it up, yes. Otherwise we'd never get through it. But neither of us completely skips over any of it."

"Ever notice any time discrepancies? For example, the timestamp on one camera is ahead or behind another?"

"No ... but I don't think either of us has ever thought to compare. I know I haven't, and I'm sure if Lena noticed anything, she would have said so." I paused, considering. "And if what you're saying is true, that person would have the ability to stop and start all of them at once, anyway, correct?"

"That's correct. Once they get in, the possibilities are endless."

"In which case all the timestamps would match, even if they'd been paused and restarted."

"That's also correct."

"That could explain why we're not seeing anything on the cameras," I said, "but Bill ..."

"Yes?"

"How would someone have known about Ernie? I mean, all they'd know from watching our surveillance tapes is that squirrels crawl all over the camera in the pecan grove. But they wouldn't have known Lena had a favorite unless …"

"Unless someone heard her talking about him," Bill finished for me. "You need to reset everything—passwords to your security system, phones, computers, everything—right now. Turn off your mics and disable and delete all your digital assistants and apps. Is your security system encrypted?"

"It came with two-fifty-six-bit AES encryption, which I know virtually nothing about, but they assured me that would keep it safe."

"In most cases, it would. But this isn't most cases. If someone has in fact hacked in, that someone isn't some kid living in his parents' basement. You're going to need to go a step beyond safe. Call your company as soon as they open and ask about end-to-end encryption. And Brian ..."

"Yes?"

"You're working long hours. Lena needs to come stay with us until we get this figured out."

It was as if he'd read my mind. "I agree, Bill, and thank you." I was glad I hadn't had a chance to indulge in the Scotch, although it certainly would have gone down smoothly at that moment.

"I'd like her to get here sooner rather than later. Like tonight. You, too, if you're willing. We have a couple of spare bedrooms the grandkids stay in when they come to visit. You're both welcome to them."

"I appreciate the offer, Bill, but I've apparently got some things here I need to do. I'm not worried about me, but I am worried about Lena."

"You're going to have to tell her about Ernie."

"I know." The thought filled me with dread. "That's going to break her heart. All right, then. I'll go tell her to pack some clothes, at least enough for the rest of the week. She'll probably argue with me, but I know she's been nervous lately. I've seen her checking and rechecking locks and windows. It'll be good for her to feel safe while we get to the bottom of this. I'll follow her out tonight and see her get settled in."

"I'll let Patty know you're on your way. Bring whatever I'll need to get into your place. I'm going to do a sweep of it tomorrow."

"You think we've been bugged?"

"I think there's something strange going on and we need to investigate all angles."

"Thanks, Bill. This means a lot to me. To both of us."

"Just get her out here as soon as you can," he said, "and know there's room for you, too, if you change your mind. What's that?" I heard a muffled voice in the background before Bill came back on. "Patty says be careful driving this late. There are a lot of deer out in that area."

The connection ended, and I stood to go find Lena. I wasn't looking forward to the conversation, but I was eager to get Lena safely delivered to Bill and Patty.

Part 4: The (Almost) Resolution

Chapter 37: Attorney Consult

"HEATHER CONFIDED IN Mrs. Stein." I had been leaning against the wall, too amped up to sit, while I waited for the guard to bring John to me. I announced my news as soon as he was seated, then sat across from him, scrutinizing his face for a reaction.

He immediately sat straight up, propelling himself forward, staring at me from between those shaggy curls. His eyes were huge, the irises assuming the silver quality I'd noticed so many months before, the unusual color never failing to give me pause. His face was pale in the harsh glow of the fluorescent lights, one of which flickered and buzzed continuously and annoyingly over our heads. He gripped the table in front of him, the cuffs he'd been required to wear since the chair-throwing incident jingling in the quiet room, the merry bell-sound of the chain horrifically incongruent and out of place given the setting and the topic at hand.

"She did?"

I honestly hadn't had a clue how John might react to my news, which is one of the reasons I decided to dump it on him without warning. Well, that, and I was just too damned tired to pussyfoot around. Mostly, though, I was going for shock value, hoping he'd respond without thinking, before he had a chance to put up his guard. That had worked with John in the past; he was too young and inexperienced to react to unexpected news with caution. It looked as if my strategy had once again paid off.

"She did. It was only a matter of time before DNA told us the truth, anyway."

He sat back, exhaling loudly. "So you know—?"

"Ginnis is the father." I completed the sentence for him, the words sour on my tongue, then clamped my mouth shut. I had to work to keep my anger at bay; it wasn't easy. That poor, innocent, violated girl who'd thrown up on my shoes; that poor naïve boy who'd done his best to shoulder some of her burden. I had no words for the feelings and thoughts I harbored about the monster who'd put them in that position.

Proving once again that her days were every bit as long as mine, Kathy Stein had called me an hour earlier, just as I'd stepped out of the shower and before the sun was fully up. I'd had very little sleep after following Lena to the Frazier's house and driving home again, but I needed to get in an early visit with John before court. I still hadn't had a chance to talk with him about the possibility of him crossing paths with Danny Peterson the day of the murder, and I had been anxious to have that conversation.

At Kathy's news, I'd once again relegated that conversation to the back burner. I quickly dressed and put in a call to Bill before skipping breakfast and heading straight to the juvenile detention center even earlier than I'd planned. I had anticipated pushback against my early visit—night staff was just switching to day—but I didn't encounter any. Maybe it was my expression, or maybe it was because Mrs. Stein had already set the slow wheels of justice in motion; whatever the reason, John was escorted in within five minutes my arrival.

Sitting across from me, John's only reaction to my mention of Ginnis was the snorting sound he often made. I glared at him, furious, only to realize this time the snort wasn't a sound of derision; it was an attempt to stifle a sob. Before I fully realized what I was doing, I'd rounded the table and gently turned his chair around so I could squat in front of him. He sat slightly bent at the waist, cuffed hands covering his face. I leaned forward onto my knees, over his lap, to wrap my arms around him. He stiffened, the effect of which was to bring me back to my senses.

This boy had been through a lifetime of trauma. Embracing him without permission would no doubt be triggering for him. I cursed myself. Damn it, I *knew* better. My actions had been grossly inappropriate. For some reason, his cries had called forth such a protective instinct in me I'd reacted without thinking, but that didn't make it excusable. I shifted to remove my arms, an apology already forming, but before I could pull away he fell against me, pressing his face into my chest, his wails muffled both by his hands and the folds of my shirt.

I hesitated an instant before tightening my arms again and drawing him close. We sat that way while guards went about their duties, peeking in every so often to make sure everything was okay. We sat that way while the malfunctioning light overhead finally dimmed and fell silent. We sat that way while my legs fell asleep underneath me and the muscles in my back began to quiver; while around us the troubled youth of the great state of Tennessee began to awaken and stir; while John's cries faded to snuffles and finally to steady breaths that warmed the front of my neck as his curls tickled my chin.

When he eventually moved away from me I sat back, nearly falling on my behind before regaining my balance and lowering myself more gently to the floor, where I sat looking up at him. He refused to return my gaze, keeping his head down while swiping at his nose with his wrists.

"We'll talk after court?" I asked. He nodded, and I slowly stood, pulling myself up by the table and hoping my blood-starved legs would hold me. I placed a hand on the top of his head before walking back to my chair to retrieve my jacket.

He stood, too, as I motioned for the guard to take him back to his room. He didn't look at me until he'd nearly reached the door, where he paused and shot me a look over his shoulder, his eyes swollen, the silver having turned to dark gray.

"Thanks, Brian." His voice was husky.

"Anytime, buddy."

"I don't know if he did it. Killed Faith, I mean. I know he ... did that ..." He took a deep breath. "I know he did that to Heather. That's why I bought the knife. I wanted to keep him from doing it again. But I'm not sure which of them used it to kill Faith. I would never have hurt Faith, Brian. Not even when I was mad at her."

"I know that John. You said you don't know which of them. Which of who? Do you mean Danny?

You were there when it happened, weren't you?" I seized the opening.

He looked down at the floor, nodding once. "Not exactly, but sort of. I'm tired. Like, really, really tired." His fatigue was evident, the hollows beneath his eyes nearly purple in the shadow of his hair. "And I have to get dressed for court. I'll tell you everything I know later. I promise. As long as you promise Heather is safe."

"She is."

"*Promise.*"

"I promise. Heather and the baby are safe, and Ginnis will be gone for a long, long time." He looked up and squinted at me. Apparently satisfied with what he saw, he nodded and followed the guard out of the room.

I stood in the doorway and watched his slow shuffle down the hall until he and the guard turned the corner and moved out of sight. We had much to discuss, but it would have to wait. We both had to prepare for court, and John was too emotionally fragile for more just then, anyway. To be perfectly honest, so was I. I put my hand to my shirt, still wet from John's tears, and stared at the corner around which he'd disappeared, then at the empty space he'd left behind.

We had a long day ahead of us, and I was tired, too.

Like, really, really tired.

Chapter 38: Lena

PEOPLE HAVE ALL sorts of ways of hurting each other, but to hurt an animal … what sort of monster does that? The tears that had never come upon learning my family had been murdered could have filled an ocean when Brian told me about Ernie. I didn't even attempt to hide them. If anyone deserved my grief, it was he.

I hadn't wanted to leave Brian's home—my home, now—but I knew it made him feel better to have me safely tucked away with Bill and Patty. And they were kind to me; they went out of their way to make me feel at home. But it still felt strange to me on multiple levels.

In my memory, the house I grew up in—the one I ran away from when I was a teen—was always dark, both literally and figuratively. My father, a notoriously stingy bastard, refused to let us turn lights on during the day lest we waste electricity. Our curtains and drapes were always closed, whether by design or through indifference I couldn't say. Layers of cigarette smoke hung in the air over furniture that bled stuffing out of ripped and torn upholstery. I distinctly re-member watching all that smoke part and swirl any-time someone walked across a room.

No trip down memory lane would be complete without the sounds. My father's voice always comes to me first, perpetually angry, berating, cursing, sar-castic. My mother's is next. Hers alternated between wheedling when she needed cooperation from my sister Callie, and irritation when she addressed anyone else. For her part, Callie squealed or shrieked or moaned, depending on the situation, always accom-panied by frenzied side-to-side rocking in her wheel-chair, the *thump thump thump* of the wheels something I still sometimes hear in my sleep. And then there was Rebecca. Her voice was angry. Shrill. Shit rolls down-hill, they say, so whatever my mother dished out to Rebecca made its way naturally down to me, double-wrapped in fury, as it were, Rebecca's anger layered around my mother's.

There was no joy in that house, in those people, in that family. Even now, sitting in my memories, I become anxious. My palms grow damp; my heartrate jumps; my stomach churns. I can't breathe.

I couldn't have been older than fourteen the first time I ran away from home. I was headed towards Richardson Landing, where Highway 59 drops right off into the Mississippi River. I suppose it must seem strange that this was where I'd chosen to go, but I'd been drawn to the river ever since Ms. Sterling, my fifth grade teacher, had arranged a field trip to Shelby Forest so we could stand on the boat dock and watch those muddy, churning waters rush past us on the way to the Gulf of Mexico, a place that sounded nothing short of exotic to my ten-year-old imagination.

I was mesmerized. I couldn't have articulated my thoughts back then, but as a young girl who felt utterly powerless, my attraction to the raw, violent power of the Mississippi was immediate. It was motion and wind and light and energy, and to a girl who'd grown up invisible, surrounded by dark, it was irresistible.

It was Bill who found me and deposited me back at my father's doorstep, the first of many times he'd attempted to rescue me by either carting me back to everything I was trying to escape, or, when my father changed the locks, by arresting me and whisking me away from the johns and drug dealers with whom I shared the bottoms. I was wise enough by then to stay away from Richardson Landing or any other named access, but no matter how far down into the bottoms I wandered, Bill always managed to find me.

I didn't blame him. I was a kid, he was a cop, and my dad was the mayor. But it was more than that, too. Bill was kind. He never stopped wanting to help, not when I was a child, and not now when I, as a damn-near fifty-year-old woman, apparently still needed help.

And so there I was, in Bill and Patty's sprawling ranch-style house, bunking in what had clearly been their daughter's room, surrounded by pink walls, frilly pillows piled three high on a rose-patterned bedspread, and a nightstand lamp adorned with a dusty white shade covered in fuzzy little pink pom-pom balls. My t-shirts and jeans shared closet space with what looked to be their daughter's old prom dress, eighties-style, with pink tulle ruffles pushing against the door. My hiking boots snuggled up close to a pair of fuzzy bunny slippers stowed underneath the dress.

God help me, it was almost enough to send me back down to the bottoms.

Brian had laughed when he carried my suitcase in and those were the words I whispered in his ear. "It's just for a little while," he'd whispered back, "just to be safe. Why don't you try to enjoy it? Think of it this way: you're finally getting to live the adolescent years you never had."

"Pink tulle, Brian. I can't sleep with that monstrosity hanging in the closet just waiting to slither out and suffocate me."

"Give it a week," he'd said. "Let me get our security squared away again before you come home."

I didn't mean to sound ungrateful, and Brian was right; that was the sort of room I'd dreamed about as a child, cotton-candy pink with ruffles and lace. But that time was long gone, and what would have comforted me then suffocated me now, no matter that it was light instead of dark, cheerful instead of gloomy. The feeling of confinement was the same, and it only increased when I awakened the next morning to pancakes and an array of fresh berries served on Patty's gold-trimmed, hand-painted China with a dollop of chilled homemade whipped cream topping it all off. A matching cup and saucer with an elegant silver spoon completed the ensemble.

A handwritten note on pastel flowered stationery sat propped against the coffee cup. Patty welcomed me to their home again and told me to help myself to anything I needed. She was volunteering at the library, but would see me that evening.

I picked at my food for a good ten minutes before dumping it down the disposal and setting about cleaning the kitchen, taking care with the delicate place setting as I tried to talk myself into feeling what I knew I should feel: gratitude, comfort, affection.

Dr. Lewis, the therapist I'd worked with—well, *worked with* might be a bit generous, since I was disinclined to *work with* anyone back then—once told me that familial love is so important to development that children who grow up without it often spend the entirety of their adult lives looking for it in all the wrong places. I could see how she might be right. All of us down there, the bottom-dwellers, Rebecca used to call us, were looking for some sort of connection. We found it, too, but probably not in ways Dr. Lewis would have recommended. Upon further reflection, I supposed that was her point.

But sometimes people change, even people like me who'd spent far too many years wanting what I couldn't have. I no longer wanted to be a part of a traditional family. I didn't want to feel beholden to anyone. That was one of the things Brian understood so well about me. He allowed me to define my own space—space without tulle and ruffles and hand-painted China and homemade whipped cream and obligations and expectations. Obligations, expectations, and I didn't have a great track record, and I didn't want to disappoint Patty and Bill. I needed to go home.

This was the argument I practiced as I drove to work that morning. I had it memorized by the time I locked my purse in my desk drawer and walked down the hall to Brian's office. I'd seen his car in the parking garage, and his door was open and the light was on. I knocked on the frame lightly before stepping in, my lips already forming his name, but one look at him and all those words I'd planned to say disappeared.

"Brian? What the hell happened to you? One night without me and this is what you've become?" He was leaned as far back in his desk chair as was possible without tipping over, his eyes closed, feet propped on the desk. His pants had lost the crease at the knees, his tie was stained and wrinkled, and the front of his untucked shirt was covered in—well, I couldn't even begin to guess what *that* was. Instead of an impeccably dressed attorney, he looked like someone who should be panhandling for drug money somewhere off Second Street.

At the sound of my voice he lurched forward, his eyes popping open, feet thudding to the floor. "What time is it? Did I oversleep?" He grabbed his cell phone off the desk. "Oh, thank God. I still have a few minutes." He sank back, scrubbing his face with his hands.

I stepped out to grab a dishcloth, wetting it liberally under the faucet of the break room, then returned. "Let me see if I can get you cleaned up and de-wrinkled. Sorry, but this is the best I've got," I said, as the cold rag seeped water through the front of his shirt and he shivered. "You don't have time for me to warm it up."

"You don't need to do this, Lena. I'll get it." He gently pushed my hands away. "I just needed to rest a few minutes first."

"Brian." I stared at him until he looked at me. "Let go and be still so I can get this." He relaxed, releasing my hands and sinking back into his chair. "That's better. But … what *is* this?"

He looked down. "Oh. Nothing. It's not important. Bit of a rough meeting with John this morning. Heather confessed to Mrs. Stein that Ginnis had raped her."

"I see." For nearly anyone else the news would have been shocking, but given my own history, what I felt was a sad sense of confirmation, and buried under that, a longstanding, slow-burning anger that frequently threatened to break loose even after all the years I'd spent tamping it down. *Well, of course he did. Now it makes sense.* "Was John surprised?"

Brian shook his head. "No. He knew. But he's not sure which one killed Faith."

"Which one of what?"

"That's what he promised to tell me later today. We ran out of time. And energy."

"And until then?"

"Until then, we forge ahead. Am I ready to forge yet?"

I stood back to get a good look at his shirt and tie. "More ready than you were, at least. If everything dries before you get there and you keep your jacket on, you'll probably be okay."

"Thanks, Lena. I'll go wash my face and be on my way. I've got a long day of court, and obviously a late meeting with John. Oh, and they'll be taking a look at our security system today and doing that end-to-end encrypt-a-whatever thing Bill told me to have them do."

"Does this mean I can come home? I didn't get a wink of sleep with that prom dress scratching at the closet door." That earned me a shadow of a smile.

"Let's see where we are at the end of the day. They'll call me when they know something. If I can't answer, they'll call you. You're my backup."

"That I am," I said. "Now go wash up. Don't forget your hair. It's looking a bit windblown."

"I appreciate the reminder. I'll call you if I hear anything, and you do the same, okay?"

"Will do. And Brian?"

"Yes?"

"It was a booger, wasn't it?"

"What?"

"On your shirt. It was a booger."

"I ..." He scratched the back of his head the way he always does when he doesn't want to answer right away, looked down at his shirt, then back up at me. "Yes, I suspect it was."

"Wonderful."

He grinned, the sight a relief after the mess he'd been just a few minutes earlier. "And just think," he said, "it's only eight o'clock in the morning. We have the whole day ahead of us to fill with new and interesting adventures."

Chapter 39: Trial Transcript

Defense Attorney: Dr. Long, would you list your credentials and job responsibilities for the Court, please?

Dr. Hugh Long: I'm a general practitioner and a trained forensic examiner. I received my medical degree from the University of Tennessee in 1990. When requested, I work with the police department to conduct physical examinations of the suspects of specific crimes. Sometimes, depending on the circumstances, I'm called as an expert witness for either the prosecution or the defense in a criminal trial.

Defense Attorney: You were contacted by my office to conduct an exam of the defendant, correct?

Dr. Hugh Long: I was.

Defense Attorney: Did Mr. Woods and his caseworker Kathy Stein consent to that examination?

Dr. Hugh Long: They did.

Defense Attorney: Dr. Long, I'm showing you a document that's been marked as Defendant's Exhibit F for Identification. Do you recognize this document?

Dr. Hugh Long: It's the consent form signed by Kathy Stein.

Defense Attorney: Your Honor, we'd ask that Defendant's Exhibit F for Identification be entered as Defendant's #5.

The Court: Any objections Mr. McDonald?

Prosecutor: No, Your Honor.

The Court: Defendant's Exhibit F will be entered as Defendant's #5.

Defense Attorney: And did you conduct that examination?

Dr. Hugh Long: I examined Johnathan Thomas Woods at 9:30 a.m. on June 25, 2019. I was accompanied by my pediatric nurse, Sandra Thorn, and a medical student, June Parker, from the Memphis campus of the University of Tennessee.

Defense Attorney: Dr. Long, this document has been marked as Defendant's Exhibit G for Identification. Do you recognize this report?

Dr. Hugh Long: I do. It's the post-examination report I submitted upon completion of my examination.

Defense Attorney: Your Honor, we'd ask that Defendant's Exhibit G be entered as Defendant's #6.

The Court: Mr. McDonald?

Prosecutor: No objections, Your Honor.

The Court: Very well. Defendant's Exhibit G will be entered as Defendant's #6. Continue, Mr. Stone.

Defense Attorney: What was the defendant's weight determined to be, Dr. Long?

Dr. Hugh Long: At that time, Mr. Woods weighed 123.8 pounds.

Defense Attorney: What was his height?

Dr. Hugh Long: His height was 5'9" in bare feet.

Defense Attorney: You reported strength testing. What equipment did you use?

Dr. Hugh Long: First, we used an isometric strength dynamometer to measure grip strength, which involves eight different muscles. Fascinating that such a small movement uses so many muscles, isn't it?

Defense Attorney: Indeed. And what did you find in regard to Mr. Woods' grip strength?

Dr. Hugh Long: Our report indicates that his grip strength was just under 64 pounds, which would be considered slightly below average for his age and size.

Defense Attorney: I see. What other measurements did you use?

Dr. Hugh Long: We used the *Physical Activity Guidelines for Americans*, which was issued by the Department of Health and Human Services in 2008 to provide guidance on physical activity for optimum health. Using those guidelines in conjunction with a study released by the National Center for Health Statistics, we measured the number of modified pull-ups, knee extensions, and planks Mr. Wood could do.

Defense Attorney: Share those results with us, if you would, Dr. Long.

Dr. Hugh Long: Pull-ups and push-ups are an indicator of upper body strength, obviously. One recent study from the National Center for Health Statistics found that the average number of modified pull-ups adolescent males between the ages of twelve to fifteen are able to do is ten. Mr. Woods did eight. The average number of knee extensions, measuring the quadriceps femoris muscle group, was found to be 86 for the study, and Mr. Woods was slightly above that with 90. Planks, of course, measure core strength. The average for boys in Mr. Woods' age group is 91 seconds. Mr. Woods was able to hold the plank position for 75 seconds.

Defense Attorney: In summary, while Mr. Woods' lower body strength measured slightly above average, his upper body strength and core strength measured below average. Is that correct?

Dr. Hugh Long: That is correct.

Defense Attorney: Based on your findings, Dr. Long, would it be physically possible for Mr. Woods to lift 155 pounds of inert weight from the floor to over his head, at five feet nine inches, in order to hoist that weight into a receptacle such as a dumpster?"

Dr. Hugh Long: No. An untrained child Mr. Woods' size with upper body and core strength in his range would struggle to lift an amount equal to his own body weight over his head. It's simply not conceivable that he could lift more than that.

Defense Attorney: Thank you, Dr. Long. I have no further questions.

Chapter 40: John

I TOLD HIM everything.

I told him about Heather coming to me hysteri-cal after what Mr. Ginnis did to her. I told him I tried to get her to tell Faith or Mrs. Stein or the police or somebody—*anybody*—but she was too afraid to do it because he said he'd kill her if she told. She believed him, and so did I. If he was mean enough to do what he'd already done, he was mean enough to kill her.

That was when Faith came in and saw me hug-ging Heather on the couch. She totally freaked out, and after that she wouldn't let us be alone together, which pissed me off because we weren't doing any-thing wrong and I needed to stick by Heather to make sure Mr. Ginnis couldn't do that again. That was when we started fighting all the time, me and Faith, because I couldn't tell her what had happened and she was treating me like *I* was the pervert.

I'd already told Brian I bought the knife to pro-tect Heather. I knew I'd use it if Mr. Ginnis came near Heather while I was with her, but I had been wondering if I should go ahead and kill him before he got the chance. If Faith was going to keep us apart, maybe I should just go ahead and get rid of him so Heather wouldn't have to be afraid when I wasn't around. I don't know if I could have actually done it, but that's what I was thinking about on my way home that day. That's when all the shit hit the fan.

I knew Faith and Danny were fighting before I even got in the house. I could hear it from the front porch. I was a little surprised because his truck wasn't anywhere around, but maybe Faith had gone to pick him up. She'd done that before. Anyway, I almost turned around and left. I don't know where I would have gone, but I didn't want to walk into the middle of their fight. But I also knew coming home late or not coming home at all would get me in more trouble with Faith, so I opened the door and walked in.

I don't know why I did it—maybe because I'd been thinking about how to protect Heather—but I jumped in the middle of them, still holding the knife, and told Danny to get the hell out of Faith's house. They both stopped yelling and stared at me, and then Danny smacked me, right across the jaw. I dropped the knife and ran back outside.

At first I thought he was following me, but he wasn't. When I realized he was still in the house, I hid beside the garage and waited for him to leave. I would have called Mrs. Stein if I'd had a cellphone, but I didn't. So I just sat there and ... well, I smoked. Not pot, just a couple of cigarettes, but Faith wouldn't have liked that, either. I could still kind of hear them yelling for a few minutes, and then the back door slammed. I peeked around the back of the garage, and that's when I saw Danny walking across Faith's backyard, then cutting around Mr. Ginnis' house, so I guessed he'd parked his truck on that street instead of parking in Faith's driveway like he usually did, maybe because he wasn't supposed to be there.

With Danny gone I figured it was safe to go in, but then I started thinking I probably smelled like smoke so I should wait a couple of minutes for the smell to wear off. Faith was already pissed, and I didn't want to piss her off even more. Then I heard something else, something squeaking. I looked around the back of the garage again. It was getting a little bit dark by that time, but I could see Mr. Ginnis parking a wheelbarrow beside our back door. It was full of stuff, but I couldn't really see what. Then he just walked right in. That didn't really surprise me, because he'd done it before. That was one of the reasons Faith didn't like him.

He was in there a really long time, and I kept worrying that Heather would show up while he was still there. I needed to protect her, but I'd dropped my knife when Danny hit me. I didn't know what to do—I didn't want to go in there without *some* kind of weapon—so I just kept waiting outside and smoking and trying to figure it all out.

I heard the back door open and close a few times, but every time I looked around to see if he was leaving, he was fooling around with the wheelbarrow, either getting something out of it or putting something in it. Finally, I heard the door open and close again, and then I could hear the wheelbarrow squeaking like it had before. I peeked around again. By that time it was totally dark, but I could see he was pushing the wheelbarrow back across our yard into his. Then he pushed it around his shed and I couldn't see him anymore.

I was relieved because it was getting late and I was hungry, plus I was freezing and all I had on was my hoodie, which, I don't know if you've ever worn a hoodie, but they're not windproof. It was hella cold. I went in the back door, not even caring by that time if Faith could smell smoke on me. I'd smoked a *lot* of cigarettes by then. I don't know how long exactly I'd been out there, but it seemed like forever.

I didn't see Faith anywhere. I walked all around, in all the rooms, but she wasn't there. At first I thought maybe she'd gone to our neighbor's house. She did that sometimes after fighting with Danny. She'd go over there and complain about him. Heather still wasn't there, either, which was a little weird. I started wondering if maybe something had gone wrong at her dental appointment and Mrs. Stein had picked Faith up to go to her. I thought I might have heard a car earlier, while Mr. Ginnis was in there, but I wasn't sure. I hoped if that was the case, someone would hurry up and let me know what was going on. It wasn't like I could call anyone, because—*hello*—foster kid. No cell phone, remember?

I fixed myself a couple of bologna sandwiches and turned on the T.V. while I waited for someone to get home. There was a *Family Guy* marathon going on, something Faith wouldn't have let me watch if she'd been there, but I figured I'd hear her come in in time to change the channel or turn off the T.V. I was tired, and I'd finally gotten warm, so I guess I fell asleep. The next thing I remember was Mrs. Stein pounding on the door and yelling my name while police lights flashed outside the window.

And, well, you know everything that happened after that.

Chapter 41: Brian

I HAD ASKED both Mrs. Stein and Bill to meet Lena and me in my office at eight o'clock the morning after my conversation with John. John's story had answered many questions but raised others; not only did I need to catch everyone up to speed, I also needed help sorting it all out. I filled them in and waited as they digested what I'd told them.

Mrs. Stein was the first to speak. "If what John says is true, and I have no reason to believe otherwise, do you realize what this means?" She didn't wait for an answer. "It means I could have been knocking on Faith's door at the very moment she was being killed. I can't believe I took Heather so close to that. What if I could have saved her? If I'd just heard something, or seen something suspicious ..."

"It must have been your car John thought he heard," I said, "but there was no way for you to know what was happening. None of us goes about our day expecting that sort of horror to take place in front of us. I'm sure I speak for all of us when I say we're just grateful you left before anything happened to either one of you."

"I appreciate that, Brian," she said, "and I know you're right, but still ... One thing is puzzling me, though. John said he saw Mr. Ginnis, but how is that possible? I thought Mr. Ginnis had an alibi."

"That's a good question." Bill turned to Mrs. Stein. "Ginnis spent the afternoon with a realtor. His last appointment was at six o'clock just north of Dyersburg. He left that appointment and went to a Perkins restaurant for dinner. He has the receipt, and he was captured on camera. He didn't get back home until after eight o'clock. By that time, Faith was already dead." He looked at each of us in turn. "Believe me, I'd love for Ginnis to be the guilty one. The longer we can keep that sorry bastard locked up, the better. Hell, throw him under the jail and light it on fire. I don't care. But John couldn't have seen him when John says he saw him."

"You're right," I said. "Something isn't adding up, but I trust that John thinks he saw Ginnis with the wheelbarrow. It was getting dark by then. What if he made a mistake and it was Peterson instead?"

"If that was Peterson's truck, we saw it leave at four," Bill reminded me.

"But we don't know where it went," I countered. "Maybe he moved it somewhere else, somewhere people wouldn't see him loading a dead body into it, and doubled-back to Faith's house. That would explain the way Faith Irving's body was bound. It would have been a lot harder to maneuver a wheelbarrow— not to mention escape being noticed—had she not been tied up and covered by a tarp."

Lena and Mrs. Stein had looked from Bill to me to Bill and back to me for that last exchange, as if our words were Ping-Pong balls bouncing from player to player across the table.

"Why wouldn't Danny have told the police John came running into the house holding a knife?" asked Lena. "Not only does it make John look guilty, it has the added benefit of being true. Why did he leave that piece out?"

"I suspect he knew it would cast just as much suspicion on him as it would John," said Bill. "He had to have known the Ex Parte Order of Protection was going to come out eventually. Accusing John of brandishing a knife between the two of them at Faith's house would have meant admitting that he'd violated the order on the very afternoon she was killed. Doesn't make him look good. He wants John to be found guilty, but not quite as much as he wants to protect himself from the same charges."

"Everything points to Danny Peterson, doesn't it?" asked Mrs. Stein. "But he's so much bigger than Mr. Ginnis. Stockier. Even in the dark, I'm surprised John would have confused the two."

"If Peterson wore Ginnis' hat or coat John might have just assumed, particularly since he was pushing Ginnis' wheelbarrow. It's a stretch," said Bill, "but something's off here, that's for damn sure, whether it's a mistake or a lie or something else completely."

I remembered something he'd said months before, shortly after the knife was found. "Bill, you said Ginnis had a housekeeper on Thursday afternoons. What you actually said was that it would have been hard for Ginnis to cart a dead body around without being seen by the housekeeper. That still stands to reason, whether it was Ginnis or Peterson pretending to be Ginnis who was carting it around. According to John, there was a lot of activity taking place between the two yards, activity that anyone in Ginnis' house surely would have seen. Peterson cutting through, someone with a wheelbarrow, even a parked land-scaping truck. We need to find that housekeeper."

"Damn, that's right," said Bill. "I stopped follow-ing that lead when Ginnis' alibi checked out. At that point, there was no reason to track her down. Let me find it here." He shuffled through his notes. "Here it is. Housekeeper on Thursday afternoons, quit the job shortly after the murder, disappeared, no paper trail, paid under the table."

"Oh, my God," said Lena. "I hope she's not ..." She grimaced, looking sideways at me.

"Dead?" I'd had the same thought. "If she *did* see something ..."

"John's case aside," said Bill, "given all the activi-ty he claims to have seen, I think it's fair to say we need to pull in the police. It's one thing to have a woman quit a job and leave the area. Happens all the time, especially when we're dealing with a person who, for whatever personal reasons, prefers to be paid under the table. That sort of arrangement makes a person harder to find if they don't want to be found. Unfortunately, it also makes it more likely no one notices when they go missing. Someone needs to take a closer look. I'll make a call as soon as we finish up here."

"Sounds like a good idea," I said. "I'll be in court until noon-ish. We're recessing early today. After that, you can reach me by phone if you need me."

"Where does this leave us?" Mrs. Stein asked. "How does this impact the trial?"

"I already planned to call Danny Peterson back to the stand," I said, "but the chance of us having a *Perry Mason* moment in which he takes responsibility isn't very likely. Still, he's such a habitual liar it's easy enough to poke holes and create more reasonable doubt for the jury." I paused for a moment, debating with myself before floating an idea I'd been mulling over since my meeting with John the previous night. "I could put John on the stand. What he described seeing could certainly inject doubt."

"You said 'could.'" Lena observed me through squinted eyes. "What are you thinking? It seems obvious that what he saw would create doubt, but I know you well enough to know you used that word deliberately."

"It all depends on his presentation," I said, giving voice to my doubts. "If John can maintain his composure and hold his temper and tongue with McDonald, it could help. But if not …" I spread my arms, palms up. "If not, he'll present exactly as the prosecution has sought to portray him. And we all know that's what McDonald will push for."

"So what should we do?" Worry creased Mrs. Stein's forehead as she leaned toward me, hands clasped tightly in her lap, brows drawn close over her nose.

"I'll do a little roleplay with him this afternoon and let you know how it goes. I'm not incredibly hopeful. Whether or not he testifies, I'm considering two options I want to share with you all."

"And what would those be?" Mrs. Stein's hands remained clasped in her lap, and I was struck by how difficult this must have all been for her. A foster mother murdered mere feet from where she'd stood, one foster child charged with that murder, and another pregnant due to sexual assault. I found myself hoping she had a safe place to land at the end of the day.

"The defense will rest tomorrow," I said, "even if John ends up testifying. As you know, it's not as if we have a long line of character witnesses waiting to speak up for him. A previous foster mom, a teacher from elementary school. Aside from Bill," I nodded in his direction, "who's up first tomorrow, and Dr. Long, who testified yesterday, the bulk of our case has lain in poking holes in the testimony of witnesses for the prosecution. Option one is that we rest and trust the jury."

"And option two?"

"Option two is that I file a motion for a judgment of acquittal, preferably pre-verdict."

"Break it down for us, Brian," said Lena. "Regular-people language, please."

"Sorry. Basically, I draw up a big document that tries to convince the judge the prosecution's evidence is too weak for any jury to find my client guilty beyond a reasonable doubt. If it works, John is acquitted of all charges and walks away free and clear."

"Could he be charged again sometime later?" asked Mrs. Stein.

"No. The Double Jeopardy Clause would apply."

"What are the chances of it working?" asked Lena.

"Slim to none," I said. "Heavy on the none. I don't want to give any of you false hope. The truth is, I've never had one work. Judges don't like to interfere with the process. We have the system we have for a reason. Still, there's nothing to lose by trying. Unless one of you has an objection, that's the path I plan to take." I glanced over at Mrs. Stein, whose hands had moved from her lap to her cheeks. "Are you okay?"

She nodded. "I am. No objection from me at all, Mr. Stone. It just hit me that by the end of the week, John's future will be decided one way or the other. That's a big responsibility, isn't it? I don't know how you do it."

I smiled. "I was just wondering the same about you. When this is all over, everyone in this room needs to spend an afternoon at my place. Bring a date. I'll grill up some steaks, and you can take the boat out, fish, hike, gather pecans, relax with a drink in front of the fire. Whatever meets your fancy. How's that sound?"

"It sounds heavenly," she said with a small laugh. "Now we just have to hold on until we get there."

"I'll get the motion ready tonight and with any luck, we'll have our answer tomorrow." I looked at each face in turn as we gathered our belongings and stood. "I wonder if John has any idea the time and energy being devoted to him. This kid who believes he's all alone is not alone at all."

"I'm sure he has no idea," said Lena, "but he's worth it." She reached across the table to retrieve a box of pens.

"Indeed, he is," replied Mrs. Stein, placing a hand on Lena's outstretched arm. "As are they all."

Chapter 42: Brian

SHELBY COUNTY CRIMINAL COURT
DIVISION XII

THE STATE OF TENNESSEE

v.

JOHNATHAN THOMAS WOODS
Defendant

Criminal No.: 2:28-cr-29916-TFW

JOHNATHAN THOMAS WOODS' MOTION
FOR JUDGMENT OF ACQUITTAL

Johnathan Thomas Woods, through counsel, respectful-
ly moves the Court to enter an order for a judgment of

acquittal on all counts, pursuant to Federal Rule of Criminal Procedure 29.

I'D WANTED TO put John on the stand. We'd practiced for hours with me in the role of a prosecutor ripping his testimony apart. In the end, I'd had no choice but to admit he was simply too volatile. He couldn't contain and control his emotions; he was just too unstable. Given his age and life experiences, that was understandable, but flashes of anger and insolence would hurt us, playing right into the prosecution's narrative, more than his testimony would help. We'd have to hope we'd created enough doubt throughout the process to make up for what John couldn't provide.

I'd chosen to end with John's third grade teacher. I wanted to leave the Court with the image of John as a young boy, a child with a mop of blond curls who smiled quickly, worked hard, followed directions, and strove to please his teacher in spite of the fact his mother was absent and he'd already spent years in a series of foster homes. That was the John I saw underneath the cynical, angry façade, the John he'd been before losing hope. I wanted the jury to see him that way, too.

McDonald's cross examination consisted of only one question: "How long has it been since you've seen John, Mrs. Hensley?" His point was well made, but still, if the case ended up being submitted to the jury, I hoped the image of a young, hopeful John would remain. When McDonald finished, Mrs. Hensley stepped down.

"Your Honor, the defense rests."

"Any rebuttal, Mr. McDonald?"

"No rebuttal, Your Honor."

I wasn't surprised McDonald waived his opportunity to rebut. After all, we'd had very few witnesses and he'd scored as many points as he could while cross examining them. Without something new, he had nothing to add. The time for calling witnesses was over.

"The defense having rested," said the Honorable Judge Steven Wilcox as he turned to address the jury, "we have a few matters to discuss outside of your presence. I'll remind you even at this late stage that you are not to discuss the case or otherwise research any of the information or people involved. We'll bring you back momentarily." Once the jury had exited, he turned back to us. The sound of rustling papers and fidgeting spectators filled the courtroom for a few seconds, and then all was silent. "Motions?"

This was my moment. I stood. "Your Honor, at this time I'd like to make a motion for judgement of acquittal on all charges. I'd like to address each charge individually, if I may."

"Proceed, Mr. Stone."

I'd outlined my arguments the night before, reaching thirty-one pages as I went point by point to refute the prosecution's case, reiterating not only the information obtained through my cross examinations of the witnesses for the prosecution, the holes I'd punched in their testimony, but also the testimony provided by both Dr. Long and Bill. The lack of eyewitness testimony; the absence of Faith's blood in the car, which would have been the only vehicle to which John had access; the fact the car wasn't captured on any video that day; Danny Peterson's history of violence; the Order of Protection just days before the murder; the expectation that John's fingerprints and DNA would be on objects he owned; the physical impossibility of John hoisting that amount of weight over his head and heaving it into a dumpster; the presence in the neighborhood of a truck from Peterson's place of employment the day of the murder.

It had taken me until four o'clock in the morning to complete, and I'd had to be in court by nine, but instead of the exhaustion I might have been expected to feel, I felt the buzz of a natural high, endorphins and adrenaline coursing through me and providing the physical energy and mental clarity I needed to present my case. By the time I'd finished laying out my arguments, nearly two hours had passed.

"In closing," I said, finally returning to stand in front of my chair, clasping my hands in front of me, "for all of the reasons enumerated, we ask again that a judgment of acquittal be granted on all of the afore stated charges levied against my client."

"State?" the Court invited, and McDonald stood to take his turn.

I sat, reaching out for John, placing an arm around his shoulders. Instead of pulling away as he had so many times in our shared history, he shifted, leaning his weight ever-so-slightly against me. I could feel his heart pounding through the layers of clothing, hear his breath catch in his throat as he trembled against my side.

"Breathe," I told him, pulling him closer, bending my head to whisper in his ear. "I've got you, John. Just breathe."

And I did. Have him, I mean. I'd put everything I had into his case, but even if that wasn't enough, even if our motion was denied and he was sentenced to a life behind bars, I'd still have him. I wasn't sure what that meant, and I didn't know exactly what it would look like. But I knew I wouldn't leave him behind. I couldn't. Not because he reminded of my younger self—I'm not really *that* narcissistic—but because God help me, for whatever reason, that skinny, angry, foul-mouthed, terrified, annoying-as-hell little kid had grown on me.

Lena was never going to let me live that down.

Chapter 43: John

YOU KNOW WHAT'S WEIRD? Every time the judge
wants to take a break, he calls it a recess. Maybe it's a
recess for some people, but it isn't for me. It's not like
I can go out and do something fun; I just have to sit
there and worry about things until it's time for everyone to come back to the courtroom.

Now that I think about it, I guess most recesses
haven't been too fun for me, what with either sitting
by myself with no friends, getting into fights, or being
forced to stay inside because I got in trouble somehow. When I look at it that way, maybe it isn't so
weird, after all.

Anyway, after Brian finished telling the judge all
the reasons I shouldn't go to prison, Mr. McDonald
stood up and talked for a while about why I should,
and then Brian stood up again and said, "All due respect to the prosecution, Your Honor, but they don't
have a case." He said a few more things before sitting
down again, mostly stuff he'd said before, and that's
when the judge told us to take a recess.

Sometimes when we went for a recess the guards took me away without Brian. This time, he came with us. We went into a little room where the guards sat me down in a chair before standing back in the corners. Brian didn't sit down. He walked from the door, past me, to the wall and back, over and over again. Whenever he made it to the door, he'd look down the hallway. Whenever he passed me, he'd reach over to pat me on the head the way he does. He didn't say anything, but that was fine by me. I didn't want to talk.

I thought a little bit while I sat there, just about things like how crazy it was that I was there at all, that I was being tried for murder. Back when I was younger, whenever I thought about how my life had turned out I'd get sad. I mean, why me? I know what a stupid question that is. I mean, why anybody, right? But when I was younger, that's the way my thoughts would go. Why couldn't I have two parents, or at least one who gave a damn?

You could always tell those kids, the ones who had parents who gave a damn. When I was little, they were the ones with food in their lunch boxes and warm coats and clean faces. When I was older, they were the ones I had to borrow pencils and paper from. They had clothes that fit and hair that was cut and their moms showed up for everything—classroom parties, lunch duty, field trips, you name it, almost as if they couldn't stand to be away from their kids even for a day.

For a long time, the moms were nice to me—a hell of a lot nicer than their kids were, I can tell you that. I knew they felt sorry for me, the moms, both for the elementary-school me with the crusty nose and too-short jeans, and for the middle-school me with the shaggy hair and crooked teeth. I could see it in the way they looked at me, at least at first. But by the time I got to high school, they no longer looked at me the same way. That's when they started holding their purses tighter and crossing to the other side of the walk when they saw me coming, as if they thought I was some kind of criminal. As if now that I was older, it was somehow my fault I didn't have parents who made sure I had clothes that fit, parents who took me to get my hair cut and my teeth fixed.

It was easy to fall into feeling sorry for myself if I let myself go there, so I tried not to. I tried to be angry instead. I guess maybe I'd gotten a little too good at being angry, because that's why I was always in trouble. It's also why Brian wouldn't let me tell the jury what I saw happen. As soon as he started pretending to be Mr. McDonald, I got pissed off. I couldn't help it. I'd known too many Mr. McDonald's in my life, and getting angry was the only way I knew to keep them away from me.

Sitting in that little room with Brian and the guards, I wasn't sure if I felt sad or angry or something else altogether. When Brian finally got the call, he looked at me and said, "It's time, John," and my stomach clenched up so much I was afraid I might puke. That's when I knew I was scared. Like, terrified scared.

I tried to stand up, but everything went dark and I lost my balance. Before I could fall I felt hands grabbing me, and then I heard Brian telling me to breathe again. "Let him sit a minute," he said. "Bend over, John. Put your head between your knees. That's it." I felt his hand on my back, pushing me forward.

I sat that way for a minute while Brian talked to the guards, not about my case or anything important. Just about the weather and the fishing on Mallard Lake. He kept his hand on my back while he talked, and I don't know why, but listening to him helped. After a minute, I sat up. "You okay?" he asked, and I nodded. I wasn't okay, but I was as okay as I was going to get.

"Then let's go," he said, but he didn't move away from me to let the guards stand beside me. Instead, he helped me up and put his arm around my shoulders, and the guards followed behind us. I don't know if he was allowed to do that or not, but nobody said anything. We walked into the courtroom that way, all the way to our chairs before we sat, waiting for the judge.

It didn't take long. The dude in the uniform told us to stand up again just as the judge came in through a side door. He stepped up to that big desk he sits behind and told everyone to be seated, and then he just sat there for the longest time, looking all around. He looked all over the courtroom, at the jury, then at Mr. McDonald, and finally at me. He stared at me so long I didn't know what to do. I didn't want to stare back at him because Brian had told me not to stare, and I was way past counting to three by then. But I was afraid he'd think I was guilty if I looked away. Finally, I had to. I couldn't take it anymore, so I just looked down at my lap, where my hands were, looking at them as if I'd never seen them before. They did look kind of weird, to tell you the truth, but then, so did everything: wavy, growing and shrinking, the colors all fading out. I started to feel the way I'd felt when Brian first got the call, like I might pass out or something. Brian must have known because he put his arm back around my shoulders, I guess to catch me if I fell.

When I looked back up, I saw that the judge had taken off his glasses. He was rubbing his eyes the way Brian does when he's tired, or sometimes when he's just tired of me being difficult, as he says. I didn't know which it was the judge was feeling, but I wished he'd get on with it; I didn't think I could stand the waiting much longer. When he finally finished rubbing his eyes, he put his glasses back on and propped his chin on his hand. And that's when he finally started talking.

He talked and talked, going over the entire case, everything Brian had said, and everything Mr. McDonald had said, and everything the witnesses had said. He talked so long I started to think maybe I hadn't understood; maybe he wasn't going to tell us whether or not he was going to approve Brian's motion. Maybe he had forgotten all about it and was just getting ready to turn it over to the jury so they could vote on whether or not to throw me in prison.

But then he said, "The standard for considering a Rule Twenty-nine motion dictates that the Court must consider this motion on evidence taken in the light that is most favorable to the State, and I am satisfied that standard has been met." I looked over at Brian to see what he was thinking, but I couldn't tell. Nothing about his expression had changed. Then the judge said, "To the charge of first degree murder, criminal offense thirty-nine thirteen two hundred two, there is no review or interpretation of the evidence presented by the State that is sufficient for any reasonable jury to find the defendant guilty beyond a reasonable doubt. To the charge of abuse of corpse, criminal offense thirty-nine seventeen three hundred twelve, there is no review or—"

I wasn't sure exactly what he was saying, and Brian's face hadn't changed, but his arm was getting tighter around my shoulders.

"And so, after careful and thorough consideration of all the evidence before the Court, the motion for judgment of acquittal is hereby granted."

I might not have understood anything else he said, but I definitely knew what that meant. Brian took his arm off my shoulders and grabbed my hand. Behind me, people started to talk. The judge yelled out "Order!" and banged down his gavel.

I knew these things were happening, but it was as if they were happening to someone else, as if I were standing outside a bubble and looking in at myself sitting there. I could see that some people looked happy—Brian, Lena, Mrs. Stein—and other people didn't—an old lady wearing a long black dress and crying, an angry-looking younger man wearing glasses sitting beside her. I knew the judge was talking, but I couldn't hear what he said. I saw the jury line up and walk out, and then saw other people standing up, but I couldn't move.

Part of my brain kept telling me I was free, and I was happy about that, I guess, but another part kept asking, now what? What does freedom mean when you're nothing but a fourteen-year-old foster kid? Where was I supposed to go? What was I supposed to do? Everyone else got to go back to their regular lives, but what about me?

And then I felt Brian's hand on my cheek forcing my head around to make me look at him. He was squatted down in front of me. "It'll be okay, John," he said, looking straight at me, his face close to mine. "We'll work together to figure out what's next."

I wanted to believe him, and he looked so serious, I almost did. But I knew better. I'd heard those words more times than I could count from grownups. Caseworkers, foster parents, teachers, therapists. They meant it when they said it, but their own lives always ended up being too crowded to leave room for me.

I still had my mother's letter, and that might have helped, but I knew I wouldn't show it to anyone. That wasn't how I wanted things to go down, even though it meant Brian would move on to another client and another case and forget all about me.

Part 5: The Final Puzzle Pieces

Chapter 44: Brian

January, 2020

"DON'T BOTHER GETTING UP."

I looked up from the casefile I'd been studying to see Bill entering my office with his hands full of—

"What the hell do you have, Bill?"

"Scotch." He reached one foot behind him to push the door closed. "Johnnie Walker Blue Label, to be exact." He set a file folder, two tumblers, and a sparkling bottle of amber liquid on my desk before pulling up a chair and sitting opposite me. "Left over from my retirement party."

"What's the occasion?"

"No occasion, just some news." He busied himself pouring two generous drinks.

I couldn't help but notice he hadn't made eye contact when answering my question, but I wasn't yet sure if that was deliberate. Still, I felt a prickling of anxiety. "Should we invite Lena?"

"No." He shook his head. "She knows I'm here. She's your designated driver, if you get to that point.

Didn't you wonder about your afternoon appointments canceling?"

"I hadn't realized they were cancelled," I told him. "Lena didn't say anything. Easy on the drink, though. I stopped drinking the afternoons away a few years back."

"I remember," he said, setting the bottle down with a *thump* before sliding one glass over to me. "This here is strictly in case of emergency. Cheers. Now, what you do with the news I'm about to share is up to you, but I want to run some things past you before we involve Lena."

"You're making me nervous, Bill."

"Just you wait." He sat back, regarding me. "I haven't even gotten started."

"Then let's get to it." I glanced at my watch. If I had an entire afternoon to myself, I'd visit John in the residential facility Mrs. Stein had found. I tried to get there three or four times a week. Sometimes, he seemed happy to see me. More often, he reminded me of our early days, before the trial, when he spent our visits slouched in his seat, frowning at me through his hair. I knew it would take time for him to realize I wasn't going anywhere. I understood that, and I didn't blame him. Someday, I hoped to provide a foster home for him.

He didn't know that yet; Mrs. Stein and I had agreed we shouldn't tell him until Lena and I had completed all the necessary steps and plans were finalized. He'd had too many disappointments already. I didn't foresee anything standing in our way, but Lena was worried. I reassured her the best I could, pointing out that she hadn't been convicted and her bumpy past was well behind her. But still she worried, vowing to move out if her presence in my home became a problem. I didn't want that, of course, telling her my home is her home, too, and it would never come to that. I didn't know how we'd resolve things if her past stood in the way, but we'd figure it out somehow, in a way that kept the three of us together instead of pulling us apart. We were also hoping John would use the time to avail himself of the various therapeutic opportunities offered on his unit, but so far, no such luck on that end.

"What have you got?" I turned my attention back to Bill, eager to hear whatever he had to say and then get on the road. The facility was an hour away; an afternoon to burn was an unexpected gift.

Bill reached to pick up the file folder he'd brought, flipping through before saying, "Francis Johnson Thorne. Name mean anything to you?"

I gave myself a moment to mull it over, flipping through mental rolodexes. "No. It's an unusual name; I think I'd remember it if I'd ever heard it. Who is she?"

"He," said Bill, "and was. At least, it's assumed to be 'was,' since he hasn't been heard from in nearly thirty-three years."

"Okay, who was he?" I was beginning to think maybe Bill was bringing me a new case, a doozy, apparently, since he came armed with expensive alcohol.

He sat back in his chair, steepling his fingers, the folder balanced on his lap. "Came from a good family. A local family. Was a football hero in high school, a rival school to the one Rebecca and Lena attended—well, Rebecca, anyway—although I can't find any evidence they knew each other back then. Hell, his jersey is still hanging in Nell's Café, right over where we sat the day we stopped for lunch after the shooting range."

I'd been to Nell's many times, had always noticed jerseys on the wall, of course, but hadn't known to whom they belonged or what their significance was.

"At any rate," Bill was saying, "in the early eighties he left town and headed north to work for Miller Copper, Inc., a factory that makes copper fittings. Back then, they were known as the factory to work for. Paid hourly wages a good two dollars higher than any place around here. He was also a part-time student at Logan Community College, a little two-year college just over the Tennessee-Kentucky line. Business major. The school closed down over a decade ago. The factory is still there, although the pay isn't what it used to be. Someone else worked at that factory, too, way back in nineteen eighty-seven when our boy disappeared. Worked there until fairly recently, in fact."

"And who might that have been?" I was intrigued. Bill was clearly handing me puzzle pieces, waiting for me to fit them together.

"Rebecca Reynolds."

I don't know whose name I'd been expecting, but it certainly wasn't Rebecca's. I vaguely remembered that prior to Lena's trial she'd worked at a factory somewhere north of Owensfield, but I hadn't known any details. Still, Bill had handed me a puzzle piece I thought I could slot into place. "And you think Rebecca was responsible for Francis' disappearance? Based on what?"

He sat forward, tossing the folder back onto my desk. "This is where it gets really interesting. Francis went by Frank. To most people, anyway. Word on the street is that Rebecca's pet name for him was Adonis."

"Pet name?"

"They dated for over four years."

"It was serious, then."

"Serious enough for an engagement. Until Frank disappeared."

I'd never heard Rebecca mention a previous engagement, much less a missing boyfriend, but then, why would I have? It had happened decades prior to us meeting, and it had nothing to do with Lena's case. I said as much to Bill.

"I might agree with you," he said, "except it came to my attention that Frank Thorne was the older brother of Faith Irving."

My mind grasped at the clues, but I couldn't yet make sense of them. "Faith and Frank," I said. "Siblings. One missing and presumed dead, and the other murdered years later. Tragic, no doubt, but how does Rebecca fit into this? Even if she did something to Frank, caused his disappearance, she had nothing to do with Faith."

"I think she might have, Brian." He reached for the folder again, flipping toward the back to consult it. "On November twelfth of two thousand eighteen, Faith Irving traveled to Kentucky to ask investigators to reopen the case into Frank's disappearance. A cold case squad had just formed—it was profiled on one of those true crime cable channels—and she hoped to drum up enough attention to ensure Frank's was one of the first cases they looked at."

I gave my head a quick shake, as if doing so would sort out my jumbled thoughts. "Let me get this straight." Standing, I walked to a dry erase board on the wall behind Bill. "Rebecca and Frank both hailed from this area, and both left sometime in the early-to-mid-eighties to work at Miller Copper, Inc. They dated for four years, even getting engaged somewhere along the way." I began to sketch a timeline. "After which Frank disappeared and hasn't been seen nor heard from in the thirty-three years since. Right so far?" Bill nodded, and I drew another line. "Upon learning of a new cold case squad, his sister Faith meets with investigators in November of two thousand eighteen to pressure them to reopen the case."

Bill nodded. "Good so far."

I turned back to the board, adding another entry. "Faith is murdered two months later, on January seventeenth, two thousand nineteen. Your theory is that Rebecca killed her, presumably to shut her up so that Frank's disappearance would remain unsolved." I stood back to observe the board. "It's certainly interesting. Compelling, even. But Bill, it still stretches the imagination. Was Frank's case reopened?"

Bill shook his head. "No. As you can imagine, once that new unit was formed families bombarded the station with calls, all of them hoping to find out what happened to their missing loved ones. With Faith no longer around to drum up attention, poor Frank was pushed to the back burner again."

"Maybe, maybe not," I countered. I didn't want to jump to conclusions. I'd never known Bill to do that, either, but I was having a hard time following his logic. "We can't know why they've chosen not to reopen it, nor can we know that they never will. It's possible there were simply other cases they thought would be easier to solve, and they preferred to start with those. Regardless, we have absolutely no proof

Rebecca was anywhere near Faith. For all we know, she wasn't even in the country."

Without a word, Bill pulled a sheet from the folder and handed it to me. It took me a moment to realize I was looking at the results of a DNA test. "Whose—"

"Rebecca's," he interrupted. "One of the previously unidentified samples on the knife. Except now it's been identified."

"But how—"

"Simple," he interrupted again. "I called an old contact and asked for one more sample to be compared. You may recall Dr. Grouse testified that many of the samples left on the knife were degraded to the extent they couldn't be easily identified. Not easily, but also not impossible. In some cases, anyway. Once I provided a name, they knew what to look for. It was small, a tiny sample, but with more extensive testing, they found a strong likelihood ratio."

"But couldn't that have been—what did Grouse call it? A secondary or tertiary transfer?"

Bill shrugged. "It's possible, of course. Either way, the fact remains. A tiny portion of Rebecca's DNA somehow ended up on that knife."

"What made you do that?" I asked. "Ask for a comparison with Rebecca's DNA, I mean." I was still struggling to understand how Bill went from point A to point B. Or point Q, or wherever the hell we were by then.

"It was the last day in court," Bill said, "when your motion was granted. I saw Mrs. Thorne and her younger son, Frederick, if I remember right, sitting across the courtroom. That was when I made the connection. I'd read the name in Faith's files, of course, but it didn't click until I saw her face. I remember when Frank disappeared, how hard it was on the family. His mother was all over the local news begging for help in finding him."

He looked down, wincing as if the memory pained him. "She was crying. In court, I mean, but back then, too. Still, I almost didn't recognize her. It's been a long time, and she's had a rough life. Her husband died shortly after Frank disappeared. Heart attack. And now Faith." He stood, walking over to look out the street-side window, his back to me. "It's inconceivable that a mother can lose two of her kids, both under such suspicious circumstances. I decided right then to do some digging on my own into Frank's disappearance. When I discovered he'd been in a relationship with Rebecca, I had a hunch." He shrugged, turning back to me. "Cops' intuition, maybe. Call it whatever you want. And with the odd things happening out at your place ... Well, I decided to ask that buddy of mine to take a closer look at the DNA."

"Rebecca's DNA and prints are on file," I said, recalling the investigation into Lena, "because when her parents were murdered, you collected standards, samples from the victims and others known to frequent the house, in order to accurately record timelines and evidence." I moved to sit on the corner of the desk facing Bill.

He remained silent, giving me space to fit it all together, the sun slanting over his left shoulder and highlighting dust motes floating in the air between us.

"So we have a connection between Rebecca and Faith Irving, and we have Rebecca's DNA on the murder weapon," I said. "What are you thinking, Bill?

Are you thinking she actually committed the murder? John saw Ginnis, or Peterson dressed as Ginnis—"

"Or Rebecca dressed as Ginnis. Do you remember what Mrs. Stein said, Brian? On the day we met in your office?"

I thought back to that day. We'd discussed Ginnis' alibi, the possibility that Peterson had moved his truck elsewhere to load up the body, then dressed as Ginnis and hauled her out in a wheelbarrow, and Mrs. Stein had said—I snapped my fingers. "She said Peterson was so much bigger than Ginnis, she was surprised John would have confused the two. You think maybe he didn't. Maybe the person with the wheelbarrow was closer to the size of Ginnis. Wearing Ginnis' hat and coat, with it dark, or nearly dark ..." I let the thought trail away. "But how would she have gotten there? How would she have had access to Ginnis' clothes? To his wheelbarrow?"

Still he didn't answer, letting the conclusion come to me. And then it did. "The housekeeper," I said. "You think ..."

"I think it's within the realm of possibility that the housekeeper was Rebecca." Bill walked to stand in front of the board, making one more notation. "A mystery woman who worked under the table and disappeared once the murder had been committed."

"But how could she ... I mean, Bill, Faith wasn't a large woman, but still. It would have been extremely difficult for Rebecca to have lifted her—"

"Do you remember what her family looked like?"

At his question, the images flooded my memory, causing my stomach to clench. "How could I forget?" God knew I'd tried, but some images can't be unseen.

"It took a strong woman to do that, Brian."

He had a point. "This is crazy." I ran a hand over my face, feeling numb from the revelations in front of me. "And yet, it almost makes sense. Now what?"

"It is crazy," Bill agreed, "and maybe I'm way off base. Maybe I should have gone on and retired. Maybe Rebecca is innocent of all the things you and I have spent the last couple of years discussing. But, Brian, I don't think so. Whether she was directly involved or hired someone, it fits together too well. At any rate, it's out of our hands. To answer your question, now we let the authorities handle it. I've shared all the information I have. I just hope I can stop Rebecca from causing more harm and bring some closure to Mrs. Thorne."

"I'll be interested to see where this goes," I admitted.

Bill cracked a smile. "Even though your job stops when you've provided enough information to create a reasonable doubt? Seems like I heard that somewhere."

"I guess you've worn off on me," I said, smiling back at him. "But on a more serious note, if Rebecca *was* here, do you think she still is?" I was remembering the sunken footprints in the mud, Ernie's body riddled with pellets.

"I don't," said Bill. "The last thing she wants is to get caught. She's having too much fun on the outside. It would be the equivalent of suicide for her to come back here, especially since the police now have all the information I gathered. I suspect we've seen the last of her for a while. But Brian, that doesn't mean you can let your guard down."

"Obviously," I said. "That would be a mistake when dealing with anyone as unbalanced as Rebecca appears to be. But I suspect you mean more than that."

Bill nodded. "I can't stop feeling as if two people have to be involved. The murder itself fits what we know, or at least think we know, of Rebecca. She holds a grudge, and she's ruthless. But for the stuff out at your place, she would have needed help from someone not just tech savvy, but an expert in the field. Rebecca didn't have those sorts of skills, at least not that we know of. Stay alert, Brian. Keep the security system running, and keep everything protected and up to date." He returned to his chair and sat, gathering papers back into his file.

"This is what you wanted to share with me before bringing Lena in?" I sat, too, grateful for the solid structure of the chair beneath me.

Bill hesitated, an expression I couldn't quite identify passing over his face. "Part of it," he said. "There's more. Different topic, though, so be ready to switch gears."

"I'm not sure how much more I can take," I said. "Is this topic worse than the first?"

He pushed the untouched tumbler in front of me again. "Well, that depends on your perspective. What would you think about a DNA test of your own?"

"Me?" I was confused. "Why?"

He pulled something from his pocket. "Because the custodian found this wadded up on the floor of John's cell. He thought it might be important, so he gave it to the guard, who happens to be a good friend of mine."

"A good friend of yours. Do you know absolutely everyone in this godforsaken business?"

"Pretty near. I've been in it for a long time."

I eyed what looked to be a wadded piece of paper in his hand. "What is it?"

"See for yourself."

He handed it to me. An envelope, I saw, with a note folded inside.

"Go on, Brian. Read it."

I pulled it out, careful not to tear it. Whatever it was, it was old, the paper soft and fuzzed on the edges. Donning my glasses, I began to read.

Laughing, stumbling, dangerously drunk. A disconnected memory that floated to me after I first noticed the color of John's eyes. Where the hell had that come from, I'd wondered at the time.

Well, now I knew.

When I finished reading, I placed the note gently on my desk, removing my glasses and setting them carefully alongside.

Then I downed the contents of the tumbler in one quick swallow.

As the warmth began to spread down my throat and into my chest, I was glad to see Bill was already pouring me another. I was going to need it.

Chapter 45: John

March, 2020

SO I'M NOT really sure about this whole fishing thing. I've been out on the lake with Brian three times now, every Saturday since I came here, and I'm just not getting it. "But look at the sunrise," Brian says. "Feel that breeze," he tells me. "Smell that vegetation."

"Sunrise shouldn't be allowed before at least ten," I tell him, "and I can get the same breeze from my ceiling fan without ever leaving my bed. Smell that vegetation? You're such a dork, Brian. No one says that. Besides, all I smell is mud and dead fish."

He laughs. "How can you be my son and not love this?" he asks.

Not going to lie, that part always chokes me up a little bit. But I don't let him know that.

After the trial I figured I'd never see Brian again. When I packed up my stuff to move out of juvie and into the residential facility, I threw away the note my mother had given me. *If you ever run into trouble—and since you're my son, you probably will—find Brian Stone, it said, and get him to help you. He's a local attorney. He's also your dad, but he doesn't know it. That's the best I can do for you, kid. Take care of yourself. Love, Mom.*

I'd done what she'd said; I'd gotten into trouble and found Brian Stone. I hadn't expected to like him, but then I did. And he had helped me, more than I ever expected. That's what made me decide not to tell him. I liked it that he spent time with me and joked around with me and was nice to me even without knowing who I really was. I didn't want him to start doing those things because he felt guilty. I also didn't want him to reject me. It was better, safer, just to move on with my own life and let him get back to his.

But he didn't go away. He came to see me all the time. He and Mrs. Stein even worked out a day pass so I could leave the grounds and spend Christmas with him and Lena. You know what they did? They got presents for me, all wrapped up and under the tree. Not the kinds of presents you get for a foster kid you don't know, fake Barbies and hat-and-glove sets and remote-control cars from the sales table at the dollar store—you know I'm right—but presents like the ones I'd always wanted. They got me a friggin' PlayStation 4; can you believe that? And games. And a Neff beanie, hidden in the bottom of a stocking they'd actually hung in front of the fireplace.

I kind of started thinking then maybe he wasn't going to go away, but I didn't know that he and Lena were trying to get me as a foster kid. They didn't tell me that until the day before they all came to pick me up. The coolest part was that back when they decided to try to be foster parents, Brian still didn't know he was my dad. He didn't find that out until I'd already moved in.

It was kind of funny, the way he told me he knew. We were out in the boat for the first time. We'd gone to get my fishing license the day before, and he was showing me how to cast a line. The first few times I tried were pretty pathetic, but by the fifth time, I'd managed to get it way out in the water.

"Now we sit and wait," Brian said, "and while we do that, I have something for you. It's come to my attention that you have a soft spot for envelopes." At first, I didn't know what he was talking about. A soft spot for envelopes? What the hell? He reached inside his coat and pulled a big yellow envelope from the inside pocket, handing it to me. "Sit before you look," he said. "It's a little cold to go for a swim if you lose your balance."

I sat, then undid the metal clasp and looked inside. There were three things, and I could see right off that one of them was the envelope from my mom, smoothed out again but still wrinkled from when I'd wadded it up. I was confused for a minute, wondering how he'd gotten it. "I'll explain it all in a minute," he said, "but first, look through the rest."

I pulled out a piece of paper. It was a letter, I saw, addressed to "Brian Stone, Esq" with "L. & M. Diagnostics" in big black type across the top. I could tell it was about some sort of test results, but I didn't understand what it meant.

"I don't know this stuff, Brian. What is it saying?"

Instead of answering me, he pointed to the envelope again. There was one piece of paper left, this one just a regular piece of printer paper with some handwriting on it. *Dear John*, it said, *Now you know where you got your stunning good looks and brilliant smartassery from. Love your dad, Brian.*

You might think we started crying and hugging then, but it didn't go down like that. I could tell Brian was watching me, waiting to see what I would do, but I'd known he was my dad for years, so it wasn't like mind-blowing news to me. Mostly, I just wondered what would change. But you know what did? Nothing. Nothing at all. I folded everything up and put it back in the envelope, and Brian put it back in his coat pocket and told me about Bill finding my mom's note. Then we waited for the fish to start biting. When we got home, Brian showed me how to fillet what we'd caught, and then we cooked it on the grill while Lena fried hushpuppies.

I caught Lena looking at me a couple of times, smiling, her eyes all wet and weepy, and when I walked by her to get some plates, she grabbed me in a quick hug, but that wasn't all that unusual for Lena. I hugged her back. I'm not really a big hugger, but I don't mind it with Lena. Actually, I kind of like it. She's a really cool person.

Not long after I came to live with them we were alone together one evening before Brian got home. She invited me to look at security videos with her. At first I thought it would be really boring, but then she started showing me things. Birds, foxes, snakes, raccoons, deer. It was pretty cool what all was out there, especially at night when no one would have ever known without the cameras, but for some reason—I don't even know why—I didn't want her to know how much I liked watching it. I wasn't being an asshole, exactly; I was just being kind of a jerk. Like, not saying anything rude, just kind of acting bored when I really wasn't.

Anyway, after a while she said, "I'm not the kind of person to preach, John—Lord, if you only knew—but I want you to hear this. If you don't enjoy the little things that come along, you'll waste your whole life being miserable. And what would be the point of that? You only have one life. Take those moments of joy wherever you can find them. They're a gift." Then she turned back to the monitor and pointed out a bat swooping through the air. "I'm going outside now to see if I can spot one. Want to come?"

I'd never seen a bat in real life before, so I went, and we did spot one. A whole bunch, actually. And I thought about what she'd said. I *was* enjoying myself, and it seemed kind of stupid to pretend I wasn't. I worked on it after that. I'm not perfect. Sometimes I'm still a jerk. Sometimes, I'm even an asshole.

Sometimes, I get angry thinking about the cushy life Brian has had while I was being moved from home to home, beat up, picked on, and ignored. One time, I asked him what kind of an asshole takes a drunk woman home from a bar. He got quiet for a minute, then said, "I'm not proud of a lot of things, John. All I can do is try to be better every day." What could I say to that? It kind of wiped the anger out. For that day, anyway.

I try to remember what he said, though, about being better every day. I try to remember what Lena said, too, about enjoying things when they come along. I'm getting better at it. Sometimes I'll feel myself frowning for no reason, or giving someone a hard time when they're not doing anything other than trying to be nice to me, and I'll realize how dumb I'm being and I'll stop.

We all three sat on the deck and ate the fish Brian and I had caught that first time on the lake. Brian had a little fire pit he pulled out and we sat around that for a while, not really talking about a whole lot, just sort of relaxing and as Brian said, digesting our food. Then I got sleepy—Brian likes to go fishing at the crack of dawn—so I went in to take my shower.

It was after my shower, when I went to my room to chill out and play a video game, that I found the envelope on my pillow. I put it in my sock drawer, where it stays. Neither of us brings it up anymore, which is exactly the way I want it to be.

So now I sit in a canoe once again watching the sun rise over the lake, shivering in a cold breeze and smelling mud and dead fish and being a smartass with Brian. And you know what? Maybe, I start to think, this fishing thing isn't so bad after all. I think I could get used to it. In fact, I think it's pretty dope.

Like Lena said, I'll take the moment of joy. I don't know what'll happen tomorrow—hell, for all I know, I'll be an asshole again—but for right now, this is exactly where I want to be.

More Books by Melinda Clayton

The Tennessee Delta Series

Blessed Are the Wholly Broken, Book 1
A Woman Misunderstood, Book 2

The Cedar Hollow Series:

Appalachian Justice, Book 1
Return to Crutcher Mountain, Book 2
Entangled Thorns, Book 3
Shadow Days, Book 4

Making Amends

About the Author

Melinda Clayton is the author of two series: The Cedar Hollow Series, which includes novels *Appalachian Justice*, *Return to Crutcher Mountain*, *Entangled Thorns*, and *Shadow Days*, and The Tennessee Delta Series, which includes *Blessed Are the Wholly Broken*, *A Woman Misunderstood*, and *Child of Sorrow*. Clayton also authored *Making Amends*, a standalone novel of psychological suspense.

In addition to writing, Clayton is a licensed psychotherapist in the states of Florida and Colorado (now on retired status) and teaches in Southern New Hampshire University's COCE MFA program.